THE COLORS OF THE HEART

They had reached his car when Steve stopped short. "What's the matter?" Debra asked, and then she saw it, too. A piece of paper, stuck in the windshield.

Steve took it off and read it. Even under the dim lights of the parking lot, Debra could see his face darken.

"What is it?" she asked.

"It's nothing," he said quietly, but Debra took it out of his hand.

She read the scrawled note aloud. " 'Nowicki, you're a disgrace to all white people. What's the matter with you? Can't you find a decent white girl to date? You embarrass the entire Aryan race when you go out with a dirty—' " She caught her breath.

She was barely aware of Steve taking the note out of her hand and tearing the paper into tiny pieces.

"Are you all right?"

She swallowed with difficulty. "Yes. But, Steve . . . I don't want to go to Harry's, okay?"

He shook his head, and spoke grimly. "Don't you see, Debra? We have to go. If we don't go to Harry's, and walk in together . . . then they've won. Do you see what I mean?"

She did. She couldn't say she was much in the mood for crowded, noisy Harry's, but Steve was right.

She glanced at Steve and ing smile.

At least she wouldn't b

VIDEO High

#5: THE COLORS OF THE HEART

Marilyn Kaye

Z·FAVE
KENSINGTON PUBLISHING CORP.

For Colette Moran

Z*FAVE BOOKS are published by

Kensington Publishing Corp.
850 Third Avenue
New York, NY 10022

First Printing: October, 1994

Printed in the United States of America

One

At the little table in the cozy kitchen, Debra Lewis savored the last bite of her pecan pie. "Mm," she sighed. "If I say so myself, this is not bad."

"Not bad?" her father exclaimed. "It's superb! Delicious!"

Her mother echoed his reaction. "The best pecan pie I've ever had!"

Debra couldn't accept *that*. "Oh, Mom, it's *your* recipe. I just threw the ingredients together."

"Well, it was very sweet of you, dear," Mrs. Lewis noted.

"I thought you two deserved a treat," Debra said. "You've been working so hard this week."

Her parents didn't argue this. They always worked hard, running the two dry cleaners that they owned. But Debra knew that the past week had been particularly rough for them. Two employees had resigned, and hadn't been replaced yet. Her parents were working extra hours to make up for that.

"It hasn't been easy," Mrs. Lewis admitted, helping herself to another slice of pie.

"Maybe I can help after school this week," Debra suggested.

"Absolutely not," her father stated firmly. "You've got enough on your plate already. You don't have time to work at the stores."

He was right, and Debra knew that, though she would have made time if they needed her. But she didn't know where the time would have come from. Between school, homework, violin lessons, and her work on *Video High,* she would have had a hard time squeezing in any other activity. But even so . . .

"I feel like I'm not making a contribution," she said. "Like I'm a worthless member of this family."

"Don't be ridiculous!" her father declared. "Debra, you are the finest daughter any two parents could have."

Her mother chimed in fervently. "You're a good girl, and you make us so proud!" Her eyes went to the refrigerator where Debra's latest report card was prominently displayed. It seemed to Debra that all her life there had been a report card on that refrigerator. And it always proclaimed straight A's.

Her father continued heaping praise on her. "You're beautiful, you're talented, you've never given us a moment's worry." He took a bite of pie. "And you're a brilliant cook."

Their compliments didn't overwhelm Debra.

She was used to hearing this kind of talk from her father and her mother. As an only child, both her parents had been showering attention on her all her life. They rarely criticized anything she did, and they were constantly complimenting her.

In all modesty, Debra had to admit she deserved most of the compliments. She did work hard, and she'd always tried to please them.

Her parents were immigrants. They'd come to this country poor and uneducated, but they'd struggled to build up a business and provide Debra with all the opportunities they'd never had. They had high hopes for her, and Debra had every intention of living up to them.

"What are your plans for this evening?" her mother asked her.

"I'm going to practice violin. Then I have to type up some notes for *Video High*. And I need to go over my Spanish assignment."

"That doesn't sound like much of a Saturday night for a sixteen-year-old girl," Mrs. Lewis commented.

"It sounds just fine to me," Mr. Lewis stated. "Personally, I'd rather have our little girl here at home, safe and sound, not off carousing with some juvenile delinquent."

"She's not a little girl, George," Mrs. Lewis reminded him. "And she should be having some fun."

"Okay, you two, knock it off," Debra or-

dered them. "Mom, I have plenty of fun. And
Dad, don't worry, I haven't been asked out by
any juvenile delinquents lately." Or by anyone
else, for that matter, she added silently. But
that was nothing new.

The phone rang. "I'll get it," Debra said,
relieved for an excuse to end this particular
conversation.

"Hello?"

"Hey, it's me."

Debra automatically smiled at the sound of
her best friend's voice. "Hi, what's up?"

"You want to come to the movies tonight
with Tyler and me?"

Debra hesitated, but only for a second. "No
thanks. I've got stuff I have to do."

"Oh, come on," Sharon wheedled. "We're
going to see that new movie, you know, the
one with Christian Slater. I *know* you love
Christian Slater."

Debra couldn't deny that. He was her absolutely favorite heartthrob. But . . . "No, really,
I can't," she repeated, with sincere regret. "You
want to get together tomorrow? Maybe go to
Harry's?"

"Yeah, okay, I'm about due for a hot fudge
fix," Sharon said. "You sure you can take a
break in your busy schedule?" she added
teasingly.

"I think I can squeeze you in," Debra replied. "I'll call you in the morning. Have fun

tonight." Hanging up, she turned to face her parents' inquiring faces.

She wouldn't call her parents nosy, exactly, just—concerned. She was their pride and joy. So, along with the praise and attention, she'd accepted the fact that every little detail of her life was interesting to them.

"That was Sharon," she reported. "She wanted me to go to the movies tonight. I told her no."

"But why not?" her father asked.

Debra began clearing the table. "Tyler's going, too."

"I thought you liked Tyler," Mrs. Lewis said as she rose and gathered plates.

"Oh, I do," Debra assured her. "But he's Sharon's boyfriend, it's their date, and . . . I don't want to be a third wheel."

"They wouldn't have invited you to come along if they didn't want you with them," her mother pointed out.

"I know," Debra said. "It's silly, I guess. I mean, I don't mind being with the two of them during the day. But on a Saturday night, it makes me uncomfortable."

"You should be having dates of your own," Mrs. Lewis commented. Debra noticed that her forehead was creased with lines of worry.

"Nonsense," Mr. Lewis barked. "She's too young to be dating." But now, he too seemed disturbed, and his eyes were searching Debra's face for any signs of distress on her part.

Debra flashed them both a reassuring smile. "Don't worry about me. There's no one I want to date, and I didn't want to see this particular movie anyway. Now, you two go relax, and I'll handle the dishes." She ignored their protests and shooed them out of the kitchen.

Filling the sink with sudsy water, she plunged into the pleasantly mindless task of dishwashing. This was a chore she never minded doing, and tonight she actually appreciated it, since she wasn't really in the mood to practice her violin. Or type her *Video High* notes.

She didn't know what she was in the mood to do. Not tag along with Tyler and Sharon, that was for sure. True, Sharon was her best friend, and Tyler had become a buddy when they started working on *Video High,* the cable TV show, back in September. They all hung out together a lot.

But she recalled the lonely sensations that sometimes came over her as she sat alone in the backseat of Tyler's car, looking at the back of their heads. And the strange discomfort she'd felt in the movies or at Harry's, when Tyler casually draped an arm around Sharon's shoulders.

She shook the image from her head. What was the matter with her lately, anyway? These weird feelings . . . and they didn't only occur around Sharon and Tyler. Every now and then, when she spotted a couple at school walking hand in hand, that same peculiar cloud settled on her head.

She'd never had a boyfriend. She'd never even had a real date. But it hadn't bothered her before. She was always telling herself she was a late bloomer when it came to dating and romance. She wanted to be in love some-day, of course, maybe when she was in college. But right now, she was shy with boys. She didn't like to flirt; she didn't even know how. And it wasn't as if she had a crush on some-one special. She hadn't lied to her parents when she told them there was no one she wanted to date. Christian Slater didn't count.

Debra Lewis, you are not ready for romance, she whispered aloud. But the words couldn't erase this restless feeling.

She thought about calling her other good friend from *Video High,* Jade, and see if she wanted to do something that evening. But then she remembered that Jade had a date tonight, too.

So she spent the evening the way she spent most Saturday evenings. She practiced her vio-lin, typed up the research notes she'd gathered for *Video High,* and she looked over her home-work. At a little after eleven, she came into the living room where her parents were watching the news on TV.

"There was yet another incident of teenage interracial conflict last night," the anchorman was saying. "At Weston High, a fight broke out during a school dance sponsored by the student government. Weston officials report that the melee began when a group of black students were denied entrance to the dance by a white student council member, who suspected one of the black students of concealing an alcoholic beverage. The initial confrontation developed into a brawl, and charges of racism and discrimination were leveled at the predominantly white student government. The mayor had this to say about the incident."

The mayor came on the screen. "Interracial conflict will not be tolerated in our schools," the handsome, heavyset black man intoned seriously. He went on to talk about the need for schools to bring students, teachers, and parents together in order to reach solutions.

"Terrible, terrible," Mr. Lewis murmured. "Schools are for learning, not for fighting."

"Are there problems like that at Greenwood?" Mrs. Lewis asked Debra.

"I don't think so," Debra said. "*I've* never been discriminated against. And I've never heard any other black students complain."

She settled down to watch the rest of the program, but her mind wandered back to her mother's question. Were there problems at Greenwood?

She'd never felt that being black had created any problems for her. Of course, she knew the history of African Americans, the ongoing struggle for full civil rights, and she was well aware of the problems others faced. But she'd lived all her life in a predominantly white neighborhood, she went to schools where white students were the majority, and she couldn't recall any incidents or experiences which had made her feel undesirable. None of her classmates had ever made any unkind references to her race.

On the other hand, she didn't talk that much to her classmates, white or black. She was a loner, content with just having two real friends—both of whom happened to be white. Sharon had once remarked that Debra was probably the only black student at Greenwood who wasn't a member of the school's African American Students League.

Debra wasn't opposed to the organization— she just wasn't a joiner. In fact, she'd always dismissed school activities as irrelevant and a waste of time. She'd only become involved in *Video High* because she thought she needed *something* in the way of an extracurricular activity to put on her college applications.

Were there racial problems at Greenwood? She'd told her mother she didn't think so. But to be perfectly honest, Debra would have had to say she didn't have the slightest idea.

On most Sunday afternoons, the Stevenson family ate lunch at their country club. As Zack's father often said, this was an opportunity to see and be seen, and a politician should never pass up such a chance.

This suited the rest of the family just fine. Mrs. Stevenson didn't have to cook. Zack's sister, Emily, could meet up with the other debutantes and scan the newspaper for any pictures of whatever party they'd been to the night before. As for Zack, his chief pleasure came from his father's behavior, the personality he always displayed when on public view. In the country club dining room, Zack wouldn't have to suffer any lectures or scoldings or harsh words. When other people were around, Senator Stevenson was charming and jovial, attentive to his wife, good-natured with his children.

But on this particular Sunday, the family was not going to the country club. A little kitchen fire had closed the club's dining room for the day. The disruption of their routine had irritated Senator Stevenson. They'd eaten at home, where Mrs. Stevenson's cooking had done little to improve his mood.

Finishing his meal at the dining room table, Zack watched his father uneasily. Sometimes, when he was in a bad mood, the senator took it out on him. But Zack was in luck today. The senator had decided to pick on Emily.

"I saw a picture of you in the paper this morning. That dress you wore was totally inappropriate." He turned to his wife. "Why did you let her out in that getup?"

Mrs. Stevenson was unconcerned. "All the girls wear dresses like that."

"Well, all the girls aren't daughters of state senators. *This* girl is supposed to have some morals." He fixed his piercing eyes on Emily.

She didn't flinch. The senator's admonitions never seemed to faze her. "Oh, Daddy," she mumbled.

He wasn't finished. "And that escort you were with—I've never seen him before. What do you know about him?"

"Not much," Emily replied. "He goes to Tech. I think."

"I want his name," the senator demanded. "I'm going to have him checked out."

"Don't bother," Emily said in a bored voice. "He was a geek. I'm not going out with him again."

The senator grunted, and gave up. Mrs. Stevenson rose. "I have a committee meeting," she murmured. She disappeared from the room.

The senator turned to Zack, and Zack stiffened. But before his father could say anything, the phone rang. Zack sprang up to get it.

"Stevenson residence."

He recognized the voice of his father's press secretary. "Zack, it's Bob Andrews. Let me talk to your father."

He held the phone toward the senator. "It's for you. Bob Andrews."

"I'll take it in my study," his father said.

Zack waited until he heard the extension click, and hung up the phone.

"Zack, do you have any plans this afternoon?" Emily asked.

"No," he said cautiously. Emily occasionally attempted to rope him into escorting one of the less attractive debutantes to parties. "Why?"

"Can I borrow your car? Mine's in the shop."

"Yeah, okay." As he handed her the keys, he asked, "Were you telling the truth about that guy you were with last night? You're not going to see him again?"

Emily shrugged. "I just said that to get Daddy off my back."

Zack eyed her sternly. "Well, I hope for your sake he doesn't have any deep, dark secrets. Because Father wasn't kidding when he said he'd have him investigated."

Emily looked at him skeptically, and he continued. "Remember that girl I was going out with a few months ago? Kris?"

"Yeah, what about her?"

"Father did a background check on her. He found out that her father's whereabouts are unknown, her mother's an alcoholic, and Kris and her mother are on welfare."

"Is that why you broke up with her?" Emily asked.

"I didn't have much of a choice," Zack replied. "You know Father's position on welfare.

How would it look if it got out that the son of Senator Stevenson was dating a girl whose mother was getting food stamps?"

Emily's upper lip curled. "You always give in to him. Honestly, Zack. You're even beginning to *act* like him. What are you, Daddy's clone?" She left the room without waiting for an answer.

Zack would have given her one without any hesitation. What would be so bad about being a clone of Senator Stevenson? He was a pretty important man in this state. And ever since birth, Zack knew he was destined to follow in his father's footsteps. He just wished his own feet were big enough to fit into them.

Emily had it easy, he thought. No one expected that much from a daughter. All she had to do was behave herself, not do anything to disgrace the family, and make a good marriage. It was a lot tougher being the one and only son. His father had plans and ambitions for him. Those goals had been made clear to Zack from the time he was a small boy.

Then, without warning, a sense of heaviness descended on him, and he could feel his shoulders slump. Lately, he hadn't done much to live up to those goals.

Going to his room, he passed his father's study. Through the closed door, he could hear his booming voice, still on the telephone. He hoped that whatever the call was about, it would occupy him all day, so he wouldn't notice that Zack was hanging around the house, doing nothing.

He ambled into his room, and slumped down in the chair at his desk. His eyes went to a framed photograph of himself, shaking hands with a former President of the United States. It had been taken last spring, when the ex-President had given a speech at Greenwood High. As president of the junior class, Zack had maneuvered himself into that position, and he'd arranged for another student to take the photo. His father had been pleased when he saw it.

"Hold on to that," he'd told Zack. "When you run for your first major office, you'll use that photo in the campaign."

He had been less pleased with Zack the following September, when Zack ran for president of the Greenwood High School student body—and lost. Zack remembered, all too clearly and painfully, how his father had berated him for weeks after the election. He carried on as if Zack had permanently destroyed all hope for his future political career.

Not that Zack himself was any less disappointed. The loss was totally unexpected—he'd *assumed* he would win. Maybe he'd been too cocky, and the students saw that. Maybe he should have acted more humble. He'd had big plans for his senior year, as the most powerful student at Greenwood. When he lost that election, all those plans went down the drain.

Then there was the humiliation factor. He was pretty sure students were making jokes and snickering behind his back. He thought he once actually heard someone saying "Serves him right, the pompous ass."

He wasn't hurt by that, just embarrassed. He had no illusions about the way a lot of students felt about him. He knew he'd never been well-liked, but he'd been respected. And his father always told him respect would get him a whole lot farther in life than affection.

But it hadn't won him the presidency of the student body. And the worst part of that was knowing how disappointed his father was in him. Zack knew he wasn't the academic type, and he wasn't much of an athlete. He was a leader. Now he had nothing to lead.

There was no way he'd join some dumb club with an established leadership, or serve on some stupid school committee. So he'd joined up with this group, *Video High,* which had just been established to put on a local TV show. He'd figured that since it was new and not yet organized, he could take over, form it, and shape it in a way that would be to his advantage. Through the medium of television, he'd reestablish himself as a force, a leader again.

It hadn't worked out that way. The show had turned into a social issues program, a forum for liberals and big mouths and bleeding hearts with their own agendas. He'd managed to get himself on the air a few times, but he'd failed to get the show to go into the directions he wanted. In his father's eyes, in his own eyes, he was still a failure.

He sat there, in silence, wrapped in gloom. Then, suddenly, the silence was broken by a crash.

Zack jumped up and ran out of the room. From his father's study came a stream of bellowed curses. Alarmed, Zack didn't even bother to knock before running in.

"Father?" He saw the cause of the crashing sound. The telephone had been flung onto the floor.

The senator's face was almost purple. "Imbeciles!" he yelled. "Stupid idiots!"

Zack shrank back, not knowing who his father was referring to. At least, the plural words assured Zack that it wasn't *him*. "What—who?"

"They're telling me I can't choose my own aides!"

"Your own aides?" Zack repeated stupidly.

The senator made a fist with one hand and punched the open palm of the other hand. "Bob Andrews says he got a call from some group called the Black Caucus, wanting to know if it was true that I had no black people on my staff. Now Bob's telling me we'd better hire a black aide to fill the va-

cancy, or this group's going to raise a stink.
There's going to be some serious pressure
put on me. This group's going to the mayor,
the newspapers . . ."

"That's awful," Zack said promptly. "What
if the best person who applies for the position
is white?"

"They'll say I didn't look hard enough."
He smacked his palm again. "This affirmative
action business is taking away a man's freedom of choice."

"Affirmative action," Zack echoed.

His father scowled. "Stop repeating everything I say!" His eyes narrowed. "Don't you
know what affirmative action is?"

Zack swallowed hard. "It's something to do
with hiring black people, right?"

"You want my opinion?" his father asked angrily. He didn't wait for an answer. "It means
giving them preferential treatment. Quotas!
Reverse discrimination! It's the white man who
suffers now. You got two men applying for some
job. The white fellow has the experience, the
black guy doesn't. But you've got to hire the
black guy."

"That's not fair," Zack murmured.

"Or, there are two boys, one black, one
white, applying to medical school, and there's
only one place available. The white kid's got
the better grades, but who gets in? The black
guy. Blacks are getting preference in hiring,
preference in promotions . . ."

As he continued to rant, Zack recalled an article he'd had to read for a class. He waited for his father to pause for a breath and then he broke in with what he hoped would sound like impressive knowledge.

"Doesn't affirmative action have something to do with equal opportunity and making up for discrimination?"

"Equal opportunity," his father grumbled. "Believe me, they're getting superior opportunities now. *They've* got the advantage." He began to pace the room. "We're supposed to be compensating for the injustices of the past. They want us to feel guilty, like we owe them something." He snorted. "Well, *I* never owned any slaves. I don't owe them anything."

Zack nodded. "You shouldn't have to hire anyone you don't want to hire."

"You got that right, boy. But that's not the way these bleeding heart liberals think." He pointed a finger at Zack. "Who did you lose that student body election to?"

"Howard Weller."

"And he's black, right?"

"Yeah."

His father nodded triumphantly. "You see, it's even going on in high schools."

Zack was confused. "What do you mean?"

"Why do you think students voted for this Weller kid? Because he's black! Because if they didn't elect him, someone might think they were prejudiced." He shook his head wearily. "Even teenagers want to be politically correct."

It had never occurred to Zack that Howard's race could have had anything to do with the election results. But as he considered his father's words, he thought that they made sense. And they were oddly comforting, too. It felt good to have something to blame his loss on, to realize that he couldn't have won, no matter what. Maybe the students honestly believed that he, Zack Stevenson, was the better candidate. But they'd voted for Howard, just to show that they were open-minded.

"They're getting everything they want nowadays," the senator fumed. "Handed to them on a silver platter."

"I'll bet a lot of other people are feeling the same way," Zack said.

His father nodded. "People are getting pretty fed up."

Encouraged, Zack went on. "Maybe you should make this part of your next platform, when you're up for reelection."

His father uttered a short, harsh laugh. "That's not very bright, son. If I had the gall to talk like this in public, you know what the press would call me? A racist."

"That's crazy," Zack said stoutly. "You're no racist."

"If things go on in this direction, I could turn into one," his father muttered. "Mark my words, boy, one of these days this nation is going to elect a president who'll have nothing going for him, other than the fact that he's black."

He sat down at his desk and began shuffling papers around. Desperately, Zack tried to think of something supportive to say, something to let his father know he was on his side. Nothing came to him.

"Uh, Father, do you need any help with anything today? I could do some typing for you."

"No, no." He turned and looked at Zack sharply. "Don't you have anything to do today? It seems to me that you've been lurking around the house a lot lately. Where are your friends? The Caswell boy, and what's his name, the red-haired one."

His father obviously hadn't realized that neither of those guys had been around for over a year.

"I don't know," he said. "It's hard, keeping in touch with the guys, when they go to a different school."

He'd complained about this before to his father. The kids he socialized with, the ones from the country club, they all went to private, exclusive schools.

"Don't start whining to me about going to a public school," the senator snapped. "I've told you before, it looks bad for an elected official to send his son to a private school. People think it's too elitist. Besides, it's better

for your future to be going to a public school.
When you're ready to run for your first real
election, you won't seem too privileged to the
voters. You might even want to start off with
a school board election."

"That sounds good to me," Zack said eagerly,
even though he had no idea what a school
board even did.

"You need to start building up your reputation now," his father mused. "Losing that
student body election was a setback. Have you
heard anything from *Metro Magazine* yet?"

"No," Zack said. "Not yet."

It had been almost two months since he'd
sent in his application for *Metro Magazine*'s
"Outstanding Senior" award. Every year, the
Atlanta publication selected two high school
seniors, a boy and a girl, who had made "no-
table contributions to their school and their
community."

"*That's* going to look good on your re-
sume," the senator said. "You'll get a lot of
local publicity."

"If I win," Zack added.

"I know the publisher," his father told him.
"And he owes me a favor or two. I've put the
pressure on. It's a sure thing."

"Thanks, Father," Zack said gratefully.

The senator picked up some papers and began reading. Zack knew he'd been dismissed.

He left the room in better spirits than when
he'd walked in. Outstanding Senior . . . it

had a nice ring to it. Yes, winning that award would please him. And more importantly, it would definitely please his father.

Two

"Good grief," Sharon Delaney muttered under her breath. She was sitting in homeroom, reading that week's issue of the Greenwood High *News*—or "Snooze," as most of the students called the newspaper. Usually, reading the Snooze *did* make her feel drowsy. But one particular article had opened her eyes wide.

"Good grief," she said again. She spoke quietly, just loud enough to catch the attention of the girl sitting next to her. But Debra was engrossed in her book, and didn't look up.

Sharon tried again. "I can't believe this."

Still, there was no response.

"Debra."

With obvious reluctance, Debra tore her eyes from her book and turned to Sharon. "What?"

"Have you seen the Snooze?" Sharon asked.

Debra shook her head. "I try not to put myself to sleep first thing in the morning."

"You should read this," Sharon stated. "It's an interview with Mr. Quimby."

Debra didn't demonstrate even the slightest flicker of interest. "No thanks."

Her lack of curiosity didn't bother Sharon. Normally, *she* wouldn't be interested in an article about the pompous assistant principal, either. But one comment he'd made in the interview intrigued her. "Really, this is incredible."

Debra issued a soft groan. "What could possibly be so fascinating about an interview with Mr. Quimby?"

"Listen to this. The reporter is asking for his opinion on teen race relations and the rise of interracial conflicts in high schools. And he says . . ." She read aloud from the newspaper. " 'Fortunately, we don't have to concern ourselves with that. We don't have any conflicts of that nature here. There is no racism at Greenwood High.' "

She watched for Debra's reaction. She expected an exclamation, a gasp, a swift intake of breath, something like that. She was surprised and disappointed when all Debra said was "So?"

"*So?* Come on, Debra. Don't you think he's being mindless? Okay, maybe we don't have fights breaking out in the classrooms every day. But how can he say we have no racial problems at Greenwood?"

"Do we?" Debra asked.

"Sure! Of course we do! Not as obviously as at some schools, but there are problems."

She eyed Debra thoughtfully. "Think about it. You hardly ever see any black and white kids hanging out together. Doesn't that bother you?"

Debra indicated the book on her desk. "Right now, I'm more worried about the Montagues and the Capulets."

"Huh?"

"*Romeo and Juliet*. We're discussing it in English. Aren't you doing Shakespeare in English?"

"Yeah, but we haven't gotten to that yet," Sharon said hurriedly. "Deb, what do you think about race relations here? You must have an opinion."

"Later, okay?" Debra pleaded. "I want to go over this before class."

Sharon gave up. Debra always put her schoolwork before the big issues. She didn't get a chance to talk to anyone about the interview until her study hall period. She'd arranged to meet Tyler in the school library.

He was waiting for her at a table there when she arrived. She slid into the seat next to him. Automatically, they both glanced to make sure the librarian wasn't looking in their direction, and exchanged a quick kiss.

She noticed that Tyler had a folded copy of the *News* tucked between his books. "Did you read that interview with Quimby?" she asked him.

"No, why?"

She pulled out his newspaper and opened it to the article. "Read what he says there about racial problems."

He read it quickly. Then he gave a shrug of resignation. "Well, what would you expect Quimby to say? Even if there *were* racial conflicts, he'd never admit it."

Sharon frowned. "You mean, you don't think there *are* problems at Greenwood?"

"Of course there are problems," Tyler said. "There's racism everywhere. But I don't think we've got anything too serious going on here."

"Think about it," Sharon pressed. "Did you ever wonder why, at every basketball game, the black students hang out on one side of the gym while the white students are on the other side? Why they don't mix at dances? They don't even sit together in assemblies."

"People sit with their friends," Tyler said. "That's only natural. I don't think they're intentionally excluding each other. Nobody's acting hostile."

"What about the skinheads?" Sharon protested. "Haven't you noticed that we've got skinheads here at Greenwood now? You know what they stand for."

"You're talking about half a dozen nuts," Tyler objected. "You can't take them seriously. And besides, they haven't done anything to anyone."

"Yet," Sharon added darkly. "How do you know what they might be planning?"

"Sharon, you're letting your imagination run wild," Tyler retorted.

As this exchange was taking place, a thin girl whose black hair was streaked with purple had arrived at their table. She dumped her books on the table and eyed them both. "Okay, what are you two fighting about now?"

"Hi, Jade," Tyler said with a grin.

"We're not fighting," Sharon told her. "We're having a discussion."

"Uh-oh," Jade said. She put her hands up, as if she was trying to ward off blows. "Let me know before you pull out the weapons."

Sharon had to laugh. She supposed she and Tyler were becoming famous among their friends for their lively disagreements. They were pretty frequent. But that was one of the reasons she loved her boyfriend. They could argue freely and openly, about everything from movies to politics, and it didn't hurt their relationship.

Jade pulled out a chair and sat down across from them. "What's it about this time?" she asked. "Nuclear disarmament? Pizza toppings?"

"Race relations," Sharon told her. "Tyler says we don't have any problems at Greenwood. I say we do. What do you think?"

Jade considered the question. "There's tension," she admitted. "But nothing out of the ordinary. At least, the halls here aren't running with blood. It's not like it was back at Hillside."

Sharon looked at her with mild skepticism and accepted that comment with a grain of salt. Jade often regaled them with horror stories of her wild life back at Hillside High, before she transferred to Greenwood. Sharon knew there was some truth to Jade's remarks, but her friend did have a tendency to exaggerate for the sake of drama.

"Seriously, Jade, did you have real racial problems at Hillside?" Tyler asked.

"There were some fights," Jade said. "We had a black gang and a skinhead gang, so there was always some sort of friction going on."

"We have skinheads here," Sharon pointed out.

Jade waved her hand as if to dismiss that. "They're not the real thing."

"They look pretty real to me," Sharon said.

Jade gazed at her sternly. "Sharon, you shouldn't judge a book by its cover."

"Oh, that's brilliant, Jade," Tyler interrupted. "Wait a minute and let me write that down."

"Right, it's corny but it's true," Jade said. "Take me, for example. When I came to Greenwood, kids took one look at me and decided I was a punk, a druggie, someone they wouldn't want to run into in a dark alley."

Sharon couldn't help grinning. "That's what

I thought, too. Until I realized you were just throwing attitude."

Jade wasn't offended. "Exactly. That's what your so-called skinheads here are doing. It's just fashion. They shave their heads and wear black boots and think they look tough."

"You're right," Tyler said. "Sharon, you can't worry about those guys. You know who they are. Denny Banks, Kurt Rhodes—they're major nerds. I remember Kurt back in the fifth grade. He was the type who put thumbtacks on the teacher's chair." He chuckled at the memory. "The jerk couldn't even think up an original prank."

Sharon had to admit that Tyler had a point. Denny Banks had been in her sociology class the year before, and he was always getting caught cheating on tests.

"They're losers," Tyler continued. "Dressing up like skinheads makes them feel important."

"But even so," Sharon said, "we have to be concerned. Remember the speaker at the assembly we had last spring, that woman who had been in a German concentration camp during World War Two? She said that people in Germany thought the Nazis were just a bunch of nuts at first. Some people want to pretend a problem doesn't exist, so they don't have to deal with it."

"And some people make mountains out of molehills," Jade said pointedly.

Sharon persisted. "Did you hear about what happened at Weston this past weekend?"

"At *Weston*," Tyler repeated. "Not here."

"Well, I think something like that *could* happen here," Sharon declared. "And we should nip it in the bud."

"My mother has a saying," Jade stated. "Never trouble trouble, till trouble troubles you."

"Another brilliant remark!" Tyler exclaimed. "Jade, you're on a roll today."

Sharon slumped back in her chair and frowned. She felt like they were ganging up on her, like they weren't taking her seriously.

As usual, Tyler could read her face, and his attitude immediately changed. He spoke seriously. "Sharon, no one's saying racism doesn't exist here."

Jade had picked up on Sharon's unhappiness, too. She nodded vigorously. "You're probably just more sensitive to the vibes than I am."

"Who knows," Tyler mused. "Maybe there's more of a problem than I can see."

"This might make a good topic for a *Video High* show," Jade said.

Tyler agreed. "Yeah, Sharon, why don't you bring it up at the meeting tomorrow?" Under the table he took her hand, and squeezed it.

Sharon's eyes darted back and forth between them suspiciously. She knew what was going on here. They were both afraid they'd hurt her feelings, and they were trying to coax her back into a good mood.

Strangely enough, it was working. Her spirits were rising. Why hadn't she thought of that herself? *Video High*—that was the perfect place to discuss race relations, to bring bad feelings out in the open, and get some real discussion going.

"If I bring up the subject, will I have your support?" she asked them.

"Sure," Jade said.

"Absolutely," Tyler assured her. Under the table, he gave her hand another squeeze. This time, she squeezed back.

English had never been one of Debra's favorite classes. She much preferred subjects like chemistry and biology, and sometimes she wondered if a future doctor really needed to know all this literature.

But this year, with Jeff Russell as her teacher, she found herself appreciating the class. He made literature something she could actually enjoy.

The young, shaggy-haired teacher was a favorite of all the students. He had an easygoing, friendly manner that made him approachable. As Debra walked into the room that day, students were leaving essays on his desk, and practically every one of them spent an extra moment or two chatting with him.

Debra joined the line. When it was her turn to approach the desk, she laid her essay down and said, "Hi, Jeff." Then she caught herself. "Um, sorry, I mean, Mr. Russell." Sometimes it was hard for her to remember to address him properly in class. As the advisor to *Video High,* he let the members call him Jeff when they were working on the show.

He smiled at her. "How did you like *Romeo and Juliet?*" he asked.

"Very much," she said. But something about Jeff's penetrating eyes forced her to tell the truth. "Well, what I understood, I liked," she confessed. "Some of it was pretty confusing."

"It's the vocabulary," Jeff said. "Many people have difficulties with that. We don't use a lot of these words anymore. The dialogue is unfamiliar to us—the grammar, the sentence structure, the way characters express themselves."

"Exactly!" Debra said. "Sometimes I can't figure out what they're talking about."

"We'll discuss it today in class," Jeff promised.

She headed toward her seat, in the back of the room. Along the way, a classmate, Steve Nowicki, beckoned to her.

"I just wanted to tell you, I thought last week's *Video High* was terrific."

"Thanks," Debra said. Then her forehead puckered. "How did you know I had anything to do with it? I wasn't on the show."

"I saw your name in the credits, at the

end," he replied. "You did the research, right?"

"Some of it," Debra admitted. "Gee, I never thought anyone actually looked at those credits."

Steve grinned. "I'd promised myself I'd write the essay for this class when the show was over, and I was putting it off. I'm not exactly a big fan of Shakespeare."

"I'm having a hard time reading these plays, too," Debra told him.

Steve made a face. "I keep asking myself, does a future brain surgeon really need to understand *Hamlet?*"

Debra looked at him with interest. "Do you want to be a doctor?" When he nodded, she said, "Me, too."

The bell rang, and she had to take her seat. She was still smiling as the class began. It was nice to find someone who shared her ambitions. Hardly anyone she knew at school seemed to have clear-cut career goals.

Jeff Russell perched himself on his desk, and began talking about *Romeo and Juliet.* "Of all of Shakespeare's plays, this is the one you folks should identify with most closely. After all, the characters are around your age, and I'm sure many of you can relate to the situation they're in."

He paused, and gazed around the room. So did Debra. He must have noticed what she was observing—that an awful lot of students looked completely blank.

"Haven't any of you been involved in a serious romance?" he asked. "Haven't you ever gone out with someone your parents didn't like?"

Debra had never been in a situation like that, but other kids were nodding.

"Then surely you can understand what Romeo and Juliet are going through," Jeff said.

One student spoke up. "How can I understand their feelings when I can't even understand what they're saying?"

Jeff nodded understandingly. "That's a good point. Although we need to learn to appreciate the beauty of Shakespeare's language, first, we need to understand what's happening in the plays. Even with the definitions provided in your textbook, the plays aren't easy to comprehend. That's why I think your next assignment will help."

He ignored the groans, and continued. "I want you to be able to see how the situations and problems described in many of Shakespeare's plays contain universal truths, emotional realities that never change. Love, hate, jealousy, loyalty, fear . . . you name it."

He must have noticed some disbelief on the students' faces. "Look, folks, these plays wouldn't have endured for four hundred years if every generation didn't find them relevant. It's the language and the forms of expression which are keeping you from appreciating the plays.

"So, for your next assignment, you will be given a scene from one of Shakespeare's plays, and you will rewrite it in modern English. I've selected the scenes, and assigned them. You'll be working with one or more partners, depending on how many characters are in your scene. And . . ." He paused dramatically, and gave them a mischievous grin. "You'll be performing these scenes here in class."

Now the groans were much louder. Jeff wasn't dismayed—in fact, he laughed. "Now, don't worry, folks, I'm not expecting any brilliant dramatic presentations. You will not be graded on your acting skills, or lack of them. But by performing your scenes in class, we can all reap the benefit of your hard work."

As he went on, Debra's insides were churning. She didn't mind the idea of rewriting a scene—actually, that part of the assignment sounded interesting. But to perform in front of the class—that was an experience she dreaded, for the same reason that she refused to go on camera for *Video High* or take part in violin recitals. She just wasn't the sort of person who enjoyed that kind of attention. The mere thought of it made her hands clammy.

And working on a project with a partner or a group didn't appeal to her, either. There was always the distinct possibility of getting stuck with people who wouldn't pull their weight.

So she waited with trepidation as Jeff announced the groups and what they'd be working on. Finally, she heard her name.

"Debra Lewis and Steve Nowicki. *Romeo and Juliet,* act two, scene two."

Debra let out a mental sigh of relief. Steve was always pleasant to her, and she'd been in classes with him before. She knew he was a conscientious student. And he wanted to be a doctor, just like she did. That meant when they took breaks from their work, they'd have something to talk about. She wouldn't clam up or get tongue-tied, the way she often did around boys she didn't know well.

She began to feel calmer. In her notebook, she jotted down the play and the portion they'd be working on. Then she flipped through her paperback copy of the play to find out which scene that was.

What she saw made her stomach go back into motion. It was the balcony scene, the famous one, when Romeo declares his love for Juliet and Juliet proclaims her passion for Romeo. And she'd have to do this in front of the whole class.

Looking up, Steve caught her eye and gave her a reassuring grin. She had a feeling the smile she sent back was a little feeble. Even with Steve, this little venture was guaranteed to provide a hefty dose of embarrassment.

Just as Jeff finished making the assignments, a crackling sound came from the intercom, followed by a hollow voice.

"This is your assistant principal speaking. I have an important announcement to make. We are proud to tell you that *Metro Magazine* has selected a Greenwood High student for its Outstanding Senior Award. Our congratulations go to Howard Weller."

Along with all the students, Debra began clapping, and even through the closed classroom door, she could hear applause coming from other classrooms. She wasn't surprised, by the announcement or the applause. Howard was president of the student body, and very popular.

The boy sitting in front of her turned around. "I think that's great," he said. "You must be very happy. Congratulations!"

Debra smiled uncertainly, but she didn't understand the boy's remark. Why would *she* be particularly thrilled? She didn't even know Howard, except by reputation.

And then it hit her. The boy thought Debra would be pleased because Howard was black.

Of course, she thought it was nice that in a school with a white majority, the award had gone to a black student. But it wasn't as if she could take any credit for Howard's accomplishment. She wondered what would have happened if a white student had won. Would all the white students start congratulating each other?

Three

Coming out of his last class on Tuesday, Zack encountered Brett Calhoun. "You going to the *Video High* meeting?" Brett asked him.

Zack gazed out beyond him, and didn't even bother to force a fake smile. "Maybe," he said vaguely. "I'm not sure. Anyway, I've got something to do first."

"I'll save a seat for you," Brett offered.

Zack pretended not to hear him, and walked off in the opposite direction, quickly, as if there was some place that he had to be. He was in no mood to get into a conversation with that little weasel. Nor did he particularly want to attend the *Video High* meeting.

All he wanted to do was the same thing he had done yesterday after school—go home, hide in his room, and mope. But yesterday, his father had been out of town. He was back in Atlanta today, and probably at home right now. There was no doubt in Zack's mind that he'd already learned the news that Zack had heard yesterday over the intercom. The announcement had been in the newspaper that morning.

Zack recalled his father's response when he had lost the student body election, and involuntarily shuddered. He couldn't bear to witness Senator Stevenson's reaction to this latest failure on Zack's part. He'd *have* to, sooner or later—but he wanted to put it off as long as possible.

With nothing else to do, he turned back, went down the hall and around the corner to the *Video High* studio. Inside, there were about a dozen students gathered on the risers. Most were huddled in groups, talking as they waited for the meeting to begin. There was no group Zack felt he'd be welcome in. But if he sat by himself, he knew he'd be the object of gossip, maybe even a snicker or two.

Brett Calhoun waved eagerly to him. Inwardly, Zack groaned. Brett had become a real nuisance. He was a clinger, a hanger-on, always tagging after Zack, trying to become his good buddy. Zack knew this was partly his own fault. Brett was in two of his classes, and Zack had behaved in a very friendly manner toward him back in September.

But that was when he'd been running for student body president, and acting friendly to everyone. Unfortunately, Brett had taken his campaign behavior seriously. He'd even joined *Video High*, just because Zack was involved. He never did or said anything at the meetings, except to try and get Zack into conversations.

Now, Brett was pointing to the empty space beside him, and indicating that Zack should join him. With no other choice, Zack climbed the risers. He even managed something resembling a smile for the gawky, pimply-faced creep.

Brett looked so pleased, that Zack almost felt ashamed of himself. He shouldn't despise the boy for idolizing him. And besides, it wasn't Brett's fault that Zack hadn't been chosen as *Metro Magazine*'s Outstanding Senior.

"What are your plans for the next show?" Brett asked when Zack sat down.

"I don't have any," Zack replied shortly.

"If you bring up any ideas, I'll support them," Brett promised.

And that would probably be the only support he'd get, Zack thought sourly. No one else in this group ever liked his ideas. Thinking about his past attempts to introduce a show topic gave him another reason to feel sorry for himself.

He hoped his lack of verbal response would discourage Brett from making more conversation, but it didn't.

"Old Hastings was really boring in class today," Brett said. "Didn't you think so?"

Zack gave a noncommittal grunt. The American History teacher was always boring.

"How did you do on your essay?" Brett asked.

That demanded a response. "Okay," Zack said grudgingly. "B plus."

"I got a B," Brett said. "Personally, I think I deserved an A."

"Hastings never gives A's on essays," Zack informed him.

"Charles Weber got an A," Brett informed him. "And you know why, don't you?"

Zack looked at him blankly. "Why?"

Brett lowered his voice. "Because he's black. Teachers are afraid to give them anything less than an A. Because they might get sued for being racist."

Zack raised his eyebrows. He'd never thought about that before. But it made sense. And Brett's opinion sounded like something his father would agree with. Maybe Brett wasn't as dumb as he looked.

Jeff Russell, their advisor, strode into the room. Zack eyed the young teacher with barely concealed dislike. There was something about Russell that grated on his nerves. He tried to be so hip, so trendy. In Zack's opinion, he was a sloppy dresser, his hair was too long, and he was too casual with the kids. Russell acted more like a student than a teacher.

"Afternoon, folks," the advisor said cheerily. "Let's get right down to business and start planning. Who's got ideas for the next show?"

A boy up front rose. "I think we should include an interview with Howard Weller. After all, he's the first Greenwood High student to ever get the Outstanding Senior award. And he's president of the student body, too."

Zack watched in sullen resignation as Jeff Russell nodded approvingly. While the advisor always claimed that the students were in charge of determining the content of the shows, he always made it clear whether *he* approved of a subject or not.

"Great idea," someone in the group called out, and this sentiment was echoed by several others. There was even a smattering of applause.

Figures, Zack thought. They're all like sheep, following the leader. They would agree with anything Russell felt. As the advisor nodded and smiled, everyone in the risers was nodding and smiling.

Well, not exactly everyone. He noticed, with some surprise, that Brett was neither nodding nor smiling. "Howard Weller," Brett muttered. The way he said that name made his opinion of the person clear.

"You don't like him?" Zack asked.

"I don't even know him," Brett replied. "But he doesn't look so outstanding to me." He turned to face Zack directly. "You know what I think?"

Zack didn't answer, because he knew Brett would tell him anyway.

"*You* should have won that Outstanding Senior Award," Brett declared fervently.

Zack shifted uncomfortably in his seat. Despite the fact that he wholeheartedly agreed, he was embarrassed. Guys weren't supposed to say things like that to other guys.

He looked past Brett at the students, who were still talking excitedly about Howard Weller. But he didn't miss hearing Brett say, "You know why he won, don't you?"

Jeff Russell was writing "Howard Weller Interview" on the blackboard. Then he spoke to the student who had introduced the topic. "Spencer, do you want to conduct the interview on the show?"

Spencer shook his head. "No, thanks. I'll be glad to help out, or do any preliminary interviews with Howard. But I'd freeze on camera."

Russell gazed out at the others. "Who wants to do the on-air interview with Howard Weller? Any volunteers?"

Zack was startled to see Kris Hogan waving her hand in the air. "I'll do it," she called out.

As Jeff scrawled Kris Hogan on the blackboard, Brett turned again to Zack. "What's the matter?"

Zack was unaware that his expression made his feelings so obvious. Quickly, he rearranged his features. "Nothing." But as Brett continued to stare at him, he said, "Well, I used to go with her."

"With Kris Hogan?" Brett looked impressed. "She's great-looking." Then he frowned. "Why would she want to interview Howard Weller?"

Zack had been wondering that himself. Kris had never shown much interest in anything besides makeup and hairstyles. "I don't know."

Jeff was now asking for more topics. Zack wasn't surprised to see Sharon Delaney stand up. She *always* had ideas, and she was so pushy, people rarely ever challenged them.

"I'd like to have *Video High* do a segment on race relations," she declared.

"Wow, that's a pretty big topic . . ." Jeff started to say, but as usual, big-mouth Sharon didn't let him finish his thought.

"Racial conflict is a big issue in high schools," she went on. "We could devote the segment to what's happening here, at Greenwood."

Jeff addressed the group. "Well? Let's hear some reaction to this."

Some girl spoke up. "But we don't have any racial conflict at Greenwood. At least, *I've* never seen any fights."

"Conflict doesn't always mean physical violence," Sharon replied. "It can be more subtle than that. Maybe we don't have seriously bad race relations here. But you can't say we have *good* race relations, either."

"She's always trying to make trouble," Zack muttered to himself. But Brett heard him.

"Yeah, I know what you mean," Brett replied. "Who says we want to have *any* relations?"

Other students joined the debate. The next statement came from the back, from Jade Barrow, who Zack referred to as Greenwood's resident punk freak.

"I think Sharon's making a good point. Whites and blacks may not have real hostilities going on, but we don't hang out together or socialize much."

"You can't force people to be friends if they don't want to be," someone argued.

Tyler Ratcliff had a comment. "But we *are* too divided here. Look at the activities and organizations. They're practically segregated."

"Is he stupid, or what?" Brett whispered. "Look at the girl over there. Unless I've gone color blind, she looks pretty black to me."

Zack saw that he was referring to Debra Lewis. He glanced at her. She was staring down at the floor.

A concerned-looking student expressed a viewpoint. "Sharon, you're not suggesting that we have *racist* attitudes here at Greenwood, are you?"

"Well, not exactly—" Sharon began, but another student broke in.

"Of course we have racist attitudes, whether

we know it or not," he said hotly. "We live in a racist society. Even our textbooks are racist."

Zack couldn't take any more. Even though he'd been determined to say nothing in this meeting, to avoid drawing attention to himself, he had to speak. "What's *that* supposed to mean?" he asked angrily. "How can textbooks be racist?"

The boy had an answer for that. "Have you ever looked closely at our English anthologies? How many African American writers are represented? And in the history books, there's barely any mention of African American contributions."

"That's true," Sharon admitted. "But if we're going to do a segment for *Video High*, I think we should limit it to our own interracial attitudes."

"But our attitudes are racist!" the boy persisted. "You can't talk about race relations without talking about racism."

Sharon looked thoughtful. "Yes, you're right. And maybe there's more racism here than we think."

"I want to say something," Brett murmured. He eyed Zack as if he was asking for permission.

"Then say it," Zack said, but he edged away a little, just in case whatever it was that Brett had to say turned out to be really embarrassing.

Brett rose. "You're just trying to stir up

trouble," he called out. Then he sat back down, looking very pleased with himself.

"I'm trying to *prevent* trouble," Sharon responded. "I know that the majority of us wouldn't call ourselves racists. But we all know that there are some students here who would. And they're proud of it."

"Are you talking about the skinheads?" a boy asked. When Sharon nodded, he said, "They're a bunch of jerks, no one pays any attention to them."

"I know," Sharon said. "And I'd like to see us keep it that way."

"I think it's time to get a consensus of opinion," Jeff Russell announced. He called for a show of hands.

The results came as no shock to Zack. Sharon Delaney always got her way. A few seconds later, the advisor was scrawling "Race Relations" on the blackboard.

Debra was wishing for a hole to open up in the floor that she could drop into and disappear. The discussion of Sharon's proposed topic was making her exceedingly uncomfortable. She had an awful feeling that everyone in the meeting was looking in her direction, taking quick glances to gauge her reaction. Like they were expecting her to express an opinion, and they were waiting for her to speak.

If so, they were all due for a long wait, because Debra had no intention of saying anything at all about the topic.

It dawned on her that she'd never realized she was the only black person who regularly attended *Video High* meetings. Or maybe she *had* realized it, but never gave it any thought. She wondered now if they all thought of her as *Video High*'s token African American. The image was not appealing. This was exactly the kind of attention she didn't like.

She breathed easier after the students voted, and the subject was changed. Two students were now giving reports on that week's upcoming program. Even though Debra had done some of the research for one of the segments, she couldn't pay much attention. She kept glancing at her watch, and wishing the meeting would end. She and Steve Nowicki had made plans to get together and start working on their project.

He was supposed to meet her here at four-thirty, when the meeting was scheduled to finish. But sometimes, these meetings ran overtime, and she was afraid the topic of conversation would turn back to Sharon's proposal. She didn't want Steve walking into a discussion of racism. She'd feel so . . . icky.

Luckily, for once, the meeting ended early. Some students left, others lingered to talk.

Sharon was accepting congratulations from Tyler.

"Well," he said, "I still don't think racism's an issue here, but now you'll have a chance to prove your point."

"You just wait," Sharon said with a grin. "I'll call you later."

He left, and when she turned to Debra, her eyes were sparkling.

"This is so super," she said happily. "I can't wait to get started."

"That's nice," Debra murmured. "I'm sure you'll do a great job."

"Do you want to work with me on it?" she asked.

Debra had expected this. Sharon always wanted them to work together. So she had prepared an excuse. "I wish I could," she said, hoping she sounded reasonably sincere. "But I'm swamped right now. There's this big assignment for English, and then all my usual stuff."

Sharon frowned slightly. "I would have thought *you'd* be more interested in this."

Debra caught the emphasis on *you*. "Why me, in particular?" she asked.

"Because you're black!"

Debra's eyes widened and she pretended to gasp. "Really? Sharon, why didn't you ever tell me?"

Sharon shook her head wearily and made a noise of exasperation. "You want a ride home?"

"No thanks, I'm meeting Steve Nowicki here to go work on our English project."

Sharon took off with Jade, and Debra moved toward the door to wait for Steve. She was joined a moment later by Kris Hogan. Like Sharon, she too looked happy.

"I'm so excited about interviewing Howard Weller!" she confided.

"Are you a good friend of his?" Debra asked.

"I've never even met him!" Kris told her. "I know who he is, of course, and I've seen him around school, but I've never spoken to him. That's why I wanted to talk to you. Tell me, what's he like?"

"I haven't the slightest idea," Debra replied promptly. "I don't know him at all."

"You don't?" Kris was obviously incredulous.

"Why are you so surprised?" Debra asked. "He's a senior, I'm a junior. We don't have any classes together."

"But . . ." Kris hesitated. "I just assumed . . ."

"That we know each other?" Debra met her eyes evenly. "Why?" She knew the answer. She just wanted to see if Kris was tacky enough to say it.

She was. "Because you're both black."

Debra smiled thinly. "Kris, Michael Jackson is black, too, and I don't know him either."

Her sarcasm was lost on Kris. She simply

looked confused. But her expression changed dramatically when Zack Stevenson approached them.

"Kris . . ." he began.

"What do *you* want?" she asked coldly.

"I have to ask you something," he said.

Casually, Debra began to back away. She didn't particularly want to hear this conversation.

"Don't go, Debra," Kris said sharply. To Zack, she asked, "What do you have to ask me?"

"Why do you want to interview Howard Weller?"

"That's really none of your business," Kris snapped. "But if you absolutely have to know . . ." She paused, and then shot him a taunting grin. "I think he's cute."

Debra had to look away, so they wouldn't see her smile. That sounded so typically Kris. She didn't care about Howard's award, or his efforts as student body president. She wanted an opportunity to flirt.

When she heard no response from Zack, she had to sneak a peek at his expression. She recalled that Kris and Zack used to date. Even so, she was a little taken aback by the look of stunned disbelief that crossed his face. He must still be crazy about her, Debra marveled.

"I have to go," Kris said, and flounced away. Zack just stood there, frozen. He gazed after Kris with unconcealed disgust. Poor guy,

Debra thought. He never got over her. It still upsets him that she's interested in other guys.

Steve Nowicki came running in. "Sorry I'm late," he said breathlessly.

"That's okay," Debra told him.

"Ready to go?"

She nodded, and they started out. She looked back for a second, to make sure she hadn't left anything on the risers, and she caught another glimpse of Zack.

He was staring at *them* now, her and Steve. And there was that same expression of disgust on his face.

It startled her. She'd never been friends with Zack, but they'd never had a nasty relationship, either. Maybe there was some sort of hostility between him and Steve.

Curious, she asked Steve as they left the building. "Do you have a problem with Zack?"

"Who?"

"Zack Stevenson. The guy who was standing by the door in the studio."

"I don't even know him. Why?"

"Oh, nothing. It's not important." She decided that maybe she'd just imagined it. "What do you think of this assignment? Is it going to be brutal?"

And as they began to discuss *Romeo and Juliet,* the image of Zack's strange expression faded rapidly.

Four

Zack couldn't move. As the other students streamed out of the *Video High* studio, he remained, staring after the long departed figures of Kris, Debra, and that guy who'd come for her. Pictures of them remained in his head, and he was trying to unscramble the images, make some sense of them.

Brett approached him. "Did you ask Kris why she wanted to interview Howard Weller?"

"Yeah."

"What did she say?"

"She thinks he's cute."

"Cute! Howard Weller?" Brett was obviously shocked. Then, the look was replaced by an expression of revulsion. "That's disgusting."

"I gotta go," Zack muttered, and he willed his legs to move him out of the studio. He went down the hall, and out the exit to the parking lot. Like a robot, he made his way to his car, got in, and started the engine.

All the while, the images bombarded his brain. Howard Weller. Sharon Delaney, chattering about race relations. Kris. Debra and whoever that guy was.

Brett Calhoun might be a nerdy wimp, Zack thought, but he got some things right. Disgusting—that was a good word for what he'd heard and observed. Kris having a crush on a black guy. Debra with a white boy. It was wrong, it wasn't natural. People should stick with their own kind.

It was the notion of Kris with Howard Weller that truly bothered him. Had she said that simply to annoy him, to demonstrate that she didn't have any feelings left for Zack, to make him jealous? But that didn't make sense. She was so pretty, there were plenty of white guys who would be happy to date her. She didn't need to fake an interest in Howard Weller. Unless she actually was interested in him. That was a thought that really sickened him.

As for Debra—that had been a shock, too, seeing her with a white guy. He'd never given her much thought before. She was the quiet, studious type who never said too much in the meetings. He supposed she was okay-looking, but certainly not gorgeous. Why would a white guy be hanging around her? Maybe he was just after some sex, Zack decided. But that was hard to believe. Debra didn't seem like the type who slept around.

Nothing, none of this, made any sense at all. Interracial dating—was this some new, hip, trendy thing to do? Maybe it was a fad. He shouldn't let it get to him. But Brett was right, it was definitely disgusting.

In his annoyance, he'd almost forgotten what awaited him at home. It wasn't until he pulled into his driveway that he thought again about his father.

By the time he'd traveled the short distance, from the driveway to the back door, his stomach was in knots and he could feel a headache coming on. He slipped in quietly, and tiptoed into the hall, hoping his father was in his study with the door closed. But as he neared the den, he heard the booming voice.

"That you, son?"

There was no avoiding the confrontation. Zack took a deep breath, and steeled himself. "Yes, sir." Stiffly, he walked into the den.

Not surprisingly, Senator Stevenson's face was grim. He stood there, in the center of the room, facing Zack as he entered. There was a pipe in his mouth, and it was clenched between his teeth so hard, Zack half expected to see the stem break off.

The senator didn't say anything right away. He was relighting his pipe, and he kept striking matches, trying to get the tobacco to catch. Zack saw that morning's newspaper lying on the coffee table, open to the article reporting on the Outstanding Senior award. From a distance, Zack couldn't read the article, only the headline, but he didn't miss the blurry photo of Howard that accompanied it.

The senator continued to suck on his pipe. Zack tried to stand up straight and keep his eyes directly on his father. The senator hated for him to cower.

Finally, his father succeeded in getting the pipe lit. He took one long drag on it, and then spoke. "This Weller boy," he said, nodding toward the open newspaper. "The name's familiar to me. Why is that?"

He knows perfectly well why the name is familiar, Zack thought. He just wants to drive home the point. But he answered the question politely anyway. "He's the guy who won the student body president election."

"The one who beat you," his father added. He puffed on his pipe, and gazed up at the ceiling in a thoughtful manner.

"Yes."

"And now he's beaten you again, I see." The senator spoke calmly and evenly, and for some reason that made him more formidable than if he'd been yelling.

Zack hastened to amend his father's comment. "Well, it wasn't exactly a race, this *Metro Magazine* award. I mean, it wasn't just Howard and me running for it, like in the election. There must have been hundreds of applications, and . . ." His voice trailed off as his father removed the pipe from his mouth, and fixed his steely eyes directly on Zack.

He made a noise, a sound somewhere between a grunt and a growl. In any case, it wasn't very pleasant. Zack knew that sound. The worst was about to come.

To his utter amazement, his father didn't choose that moment to explode. He just shook his head wearily. "It's even worse than I thought . . ."

Zack ventured a question. "What do you mean, Father?"

"Everyone wants to be politically correct these days," the senator mused. "It's the popular thing to do. Give all the honors, all the credits, all the awards to minority group members. A white man doesn't have a chance anymore."

Zack eagerly expressed agreement. "Yeah, that's it! I mean, yes, sir, you're absolutely right. I understand exactly what you're saying."

His father eyed him keenly. "You do?"

Here it was, an opportunity to impress his father, and Zack plunged in. "Just today, at my *Video High* meeting, some girl proposed that we do a show on race relations, when we don't even have any race problems at Greenwood. She was just trying to be fashionable."

"Race relations," the senator repeated.

Zack nodded and continued. "She got the group all excited. All these bleeding hearts, they were yelling about how we're all racists, whether we think we are or not. And how we need to learn new attitudes, or some kind of crap like that." He suddenly remembered his father's feelings about obscene language, and he stopped.

But Senator Stevenson didn't rebuke him for his use of a four-letter word. He didn't even seem to have noticed. "What did *you* say?"

"Huh?"

"When this girl was talking about race relations. What was your response?"

"Well, I thought she was being an idiot, of course. I felt like—"

His father interrupted. "But what did you *say*? Did you challenge her?"

"Sure," Zack said. "Well, I didn't exactly challenge *her*. But when this other kid claimed that our textbooks were racist, I said that was nonsense, and . . ." Suddenly, he couldn't remember exactly what he'd said.

"What happened?" the senator asked. "What kind of show did you decide to do? What's the topic?"

Zack's shoulders sagged. "Race relations."

His father gazed at him in disdain, as if that was all his fault.

Zack defended himself. "There was nothing I could do! It's just like you said, they want to be fashionable. The advisor, Jeff Russell, he loves stuff like that. And the rest of them, they go along with anything he approves of."

He was blabbering now, trying to get the excuses out as fast as he could. His father was now looking grimmer and grimmer, but Zack couldn't stop himself. "They're sheep, those kids, they don't have minds of their own. They'll listen to anyone—"

His father broke in. "A good politician can use that to his advantage. If you had any authority with your classmates, any persuasive powers at all, any leadership qualities, you'd know how to do this."

To his horror, Zack found himself stammering. "It's, it's not that easy, I, I can't, you know, I mean, I'm only one person and—and it's, it's . . ."

His father's upper lip curled. "I can't believe this. You're my son. You should know something about swaying opinion. Don't you have any gumption at all?"

"I tried—"

"Not hard enough, obviously. You lose elections, you've never won a single honor—"

Zack was desperate. "This *Metro Magazine* award, you said it was a sure thing!"

"I thought you were qualified," the senator declared. "I assumed I had a son who deserved an award like this. I thought I had a son who was a leader among his fellow students. Apparently, I was wrong."

He didn't sound angry. What Zack saw in his father's face was far worse. Disappointment. His next words confirmed this. "It appears that *Metro Magazine* realized something I couldn't. You just don't have it in you, do you?"

Zack had no response for that. With alarm,

he realized his own eyes were filling with tears. In a second, his father would see that too—and if there was anything his father despised, it was a man crying.

With what little dignity he had left, he murmured, "I'm sorry," and left the room. When he reached his own bedroom, he closed the door and fell onto his bed. He had never been so depressed in his life.

All his life, for as long as he could remember, he'd struggled to please his father, to win his father's approval. He even blew Kris off, just because his father thought she wasn't the right kind of girl.

He shook his head, trying to rid himself of the image of his father's disappointed face. But it was impossible. He closed his eyes, in a futile attempt to hold back the tears.

Was there any way, was there anything he could do, to win his father's love?

"Make a right here," Debra instructed Steve.

He turned the car onto her street, and followed her directions to the small, neat white house on the corner.

As they got out of the car, she noticed a piece of paper stuck under the windshield. "What's that?" she asked.

"I don't know." He retrieved the paper, and read it. His forehead puckered. He looked up, and met Debra's questioning eyes. "Just an ad," he said. He crumpled the paper and stuck it in his knapsack.

"Are you sure your parents don't mind if we work here?" he asked as they went up to the door.

"Of course not," Debra assured him. "We won't be disturbing them, they're both at work."

"But what if they come home while I'm here?"

Unlocking the door, Debra turned and looked at him quizzically. "What if they do? I'm allowed to have friends visit!"

He flushed slightly. "I just thought they might not like finding me . . . you know, a white boy."

"Oh, *please!*" Debra exclaimed. "My parents aren't like that." She smiled mischievously. "Some of their best friends are white people. Come on in." She led him to the kitchen. "I usually work in here," she told him, indicating the kitchen table. They sat down, and laid out notebooks and paperback copies of *Romeo and Juliet.*

"Would you like a soda, or some juice?" Debra asked.

"No thanks," Steve replied. "Look, what I asked before, about your parents . . . I didn't mean to suggest that they were racist or anything like that. But you know how some people are."

"Well, my parents *aren't,*" Debra said firmly.

"And can we please not talk about racism, race relations, racial conflict, or anything like that?"

She could tell he was startled by the fervency in her tone. But after that *Video High* meeting, there were certain subjects she had no desire to discuss. She flipped open her book.

"Act two, scene two, right?"

"Right." He opened his book, located the scene, and read aloud. " 'He jests at scars that never felt a wound.' That's Romeo's first line. What's he talking about?"

Debra recalled the scene before that one. "I *think* he's talking about his friend Mercutio, who keeps making jokes. He means that a person like Mercutio might laugh at him being in love because he's never been in love himself, so he can't understand how Romeo feels."

"That makes sense," Steve said. "How about if *we* say, um, Mercutio makes jokes because he doesn't know what it's like to feel the way I do."

Debra approved. "That sounds good." As Steve wrote his line down, she continued reading Romeo's speech. " 'But soft! What light through yonder window breaks? It is the East, and Juliet is the sun! Arise, fair sun, and kill the envious moon, who is already sick and pale with grief that thou her maid art far more fair than she.' "

"Whew!" Steve whistled. "Can you translate *that?*"

Debra studied the lines for a minute. "How about something like, 'There's Juliet! She's so beautiful!' "

Steve's eyebrows shot up. "That's all?"

"That's what he's saying," Debra pointed out. "What all that poetry boils down to."

Steve reread the lines. "Yeah, you're right."

"And that's what Mr. Russell wants us to do," Debra continued. "Take out all the fancy stuff and get down to the real meaning of the lines."

"He's pretty cool, Mr. Russell," Steve remarked.

Debra agreed. "He's a terrific advisor for *Video High,* too. He lets everyone give an opinion and he seems to care about what we say."

"And our class is actually interesting," Steve added. "I've never liked an English class before this year."

"Me, neither," Debra said. "I had Miss Scarborough last year." She made a face.

"I had her, too!" Steve said. "Did she make your class analyze poems and come up with a hidden meaning?"

The memory made Debra groan. "According to her, everything we read meant something else."

Steve chuckled. "Once, I asked her why these

poets couldn't just say what they mean. And she said, if they did that, it wouldn't be poetry!"

"That sounds like something she'd say," Debra remarked. "Personally, I'd rather dissect a frog than a poem."

Steve spoke with mock sternness. "That's not exactly politically correct, Debra. You'd better not say that too loud, or you'll have those animal rights people on your case."

Debra rolled her eyes. "I know what you mean. People get too carried away with their causes. I'm all in favor of animals being treated properly. But sometimes, animal testing is necessary, to find cures for diseases that hurt human beings."

"Absolutely," Steve agreed. "Personally, I don't like the idea of cosmetics and shampoos tested on animals, but if it's a vaccine or some sort of medicine that could cure a disease, I'm all for it."

"Me, too," Debra said. "Do you mind if I put on some music? We just got a new CD player."

Steve followed her into the living room. "What have you got?" he asked as Debra began going through the discs.

"Nothing very modern," Debra confessed. She hesitated. Some of her friends joked about her taste in music. "Do you like Mozart?"

Steve gaped. "Are you kidding? I *love* Mozart! I thought I was the only person at Greenwood who listened to classical music."

"No, there are two of us," Debra said happily as she put the disc on the player.

They returned to the kitchen as the sweet notes of a beautiful symphony filled the air. "What's next?" Debra asked, reaching for her book.

Steve read aloud from his. " 'It is my lady; O, it is my love! O that she knew she were!' Well, that's easy. He's saying I wish she knew how much I love her."

Debra hesitated. Was Steve the type who'd take offense at being corrected? "Not exactly," she said tentatively. "I think it's more like, I love her and I wish she loved me, too."

Steve read the lines again silently. "Yeah, you're right," he conceded. Debra was pleased to see that the fact didn't seem to bother him at all.

They continued working on that particular speech for a while. At one point, Steve flipped through the pages. "This is going to take more than one afternoon. Have you realized how long this scene is?"

"It won't be that long by the time we get through with it," Debra promised him.

"Do we have to memorize our lines for the performance?" Steve asked.

"I hope not," Debra replied. "We'd better ask Mr. Russell tomorrow." She paused. "I'm going to feel awfully silly doing this in front of our class."

"You and me both," Steve said. He

jumped off the seat and went down on one knee, with the book in his hand. In a dramatic voice, he read, " 'Two of the fairest stars in all the heaven, Having some business, do entreat her eyes to twinkle in their spheres till they return.' "

Debra had a feeling her own eyes were sparkling with glee. "Do you think people ever really spoke like that?"

"They must have," Steve said. "It's pretty, though. And I like that first line in the scene." He flipped back the page and read it again. " 'He jests at scars that never felt the wound.' There's a lot of truth in that. You know, if you haven't experienced something, you can't know what an experience is really like. And it's easy to make fun of something you don't understand."

Debra considered this. An image of Sharon popped into her head. "I have a friend, a very good friend, who went on a crazy diet once. She almost starved herself, because she thought she was fat, which she wasn't. It wasn't something I'd ever do, so I didn't appreciate what she was going through. I'm afraid I wasn't very helpful with her problem."

Steve was nodding sympathetically. "It wasn't an experience you could relate to. But I'll bet you didn't make fun of her."

"Oh, no," Debra stated. "But I wasn't sensitive to her needs."

Steve spoke slowly. "For some people, not understanding can turn into something really ugly. Like hatred and bigotry."

"That's true," Debra said. "I guess, if we can't understand, we have to learn to accept."

"Exactly!" Steve exclaimed eagerly. "Like, I could never really understand what it's like to be black, because I'm not. And I can't understand what it's like to be discriminated against. But I could never be a racist."

Debra ducked her head. "Mm."

Steve peered at her. "Did I say something wrong?" he asked anxiously.

She looked up. "No, it's okay," she said tiredly. "But I just sat through a *Video High* meeting where everyone was arguing about racism. I guess I just don't feel like getting into that subject again."

"I'm sorry," Steve said humbly.

Then she was embarrassed, for coming down on him so hard. "Oh, it's not your fault. I'm just being too sensitive. You see, the others wanted to do a show on race relations, racial conflict and all that. And I felt like everyone expected me to get involved. I'm supposed to know what racism is all about. I'm supposed to understand discrimination."

"Don't you?"

She was astounding herself, talking like this with someone she barely knew. This was like talking to Sharon! But Steve seemed so sincerely interested, so *open*.

She answered his question as honestly as she could. "I can't say that I do. No one's ever said anything racist to me. And I've never felt discriminated against. I know racism exists. I'm aware of what's going on in the world. I just don't have any personal experience with it."

"You're lucky," Steve commented.

"Yes, I know," she replied. "Very lucky. I'm lucky to have open-minded parents, and to live in an integrated neighborhood. I'm lucky to go to a school where there aren't any racial problems."

"Are you sure about that?" Steve asked. "About Greenwood not having any racial problems?"

"I've never encountered any."

Steve reached for his knapsack and pulled out the paper he'd taken off his windshield. "I didn't want to show you this. I thought it might upset you. But I guess you'll hear about it sooner or later." He handed the paper to Debra.

It wasn't a professional-looking flyer. The uneven black letters on the photocopied sheet were sloppy and amateur. But the message was clear enough.

"They're taking over!" the heading read. And under that: "Are you sick of watching blacks get special treatment? Are you tired of seeing white people in second place? Fight back! Show some pride in being a member of the white race. Join the Pro-White Union!"

Bewildered, she read it twice. "What is this Pro-White Union? I've never heard of it."

"I haven't, either," Steve told her. "But it sounds pretty gross."

"Yeah." Debra handed it back. "Well, there are some pretty sick people in the world."

"I just didn't think we had them at Greenwood," Steve commented.

"You don't know for sure that this was written by a Greenwood student," Debra pointed out. "Anyone could have walked into the parking lot and stuck these things on cars."

"That's true," Steve admitted. "But have you noticed those skinheads at school?"

"I've seen them around," Debra said. "But I don't think we need to take them too seriously."

The phone rang, and she rose to get it. "Hello?"

"Hi, honey."

"Hi, Mom, what's up?"

"Two of the staff here have called in sick," Mrs. Lewis told her. "Your father and I are going to have to work late. We won't be home for dinner."

"But you have to eat," Debra protested.

"We'll send someone out for sandwiches

from the deli," her mother said. "I'm just worried about you, what you're going to do for dinner."

"No problem," Debra said. "I'll fix myself something to eat. See you later."

Hanging up, she turned to Steve. "My poor parents," she sighed. "They're working through dinner."

"Do you want to go out and get something to eat with me?" Steve asked.

"Don't you have to be home?"

"I can get out of it," he said with a smile. "Just let me make a call."

Fifteen minutes later, they were walking into Harry's, the most popular café in the neighborhood. The after school crowd was gone, and it was early for dinner, so there were a lot of empty booths. They slid into one, and a waitress promptly appeared with menus.

As Debra was studying her menu, she heard her name, and looked up at a classmate. "Hi, Beth Ann."

Steve greeted her, too. "Did you get that algebra homework done?"

"Almost," she said. Then she looked at Debra again, in a way that struck Debra as odd.

After she moved on, Debra asked Steve, "Is there something on my face?"

He studied her seriously. "Yes. Two eyes, a nose, and a mouth."

"Very funny," Debra retorted. "I just had this feeling Beth Ann was staring at something."

"The eyes," Steve declared.

"Huh?"

He placed a hand over his heart. "Two of the fairest stars in all the heaven . . .'"

Debra laughed. "Why, thank you, Romeo."

He grinned. "You're welcome, Juliet."

Tyler usually called Sharon at ten o'clock every night. At five of ten, Sharon was watching the phone. This night in particular, she couldn't wait for his call. She'd called him earlier, but he wasn't home. Tonight, she had some real news for him.

Tyler didn't let her down. At precisely ten, the phone rang, and she snatched it up. "Tyler, is that you?"

"Why, were you expecting Tom Cruise?" he asked.

"No, Kevin Costner. Wait till you hear this. And you thought there were no racial problems at Greenwood!"

"What are you talking about?"

"There was a flyer on my windshield when I left school. Listen." She picked it up from her desk.

"'They're taking over,'" she began, but Tyler stopped her before she could get any further.

"I know, I know. There was one on my car, too."

"So you see? I was right! We *do* have problems. Tyler, this is creepy!"

"Yes, it's definitely creepy," Tyler agreed.

"Who do you think is in this Pro-White Union? Denny, and those other jerks?"

"Probably," Tyler replied.

"Maybe things are worse than we thought," Sharon told him. "Maybe there are more racists out there than we know about. If they have an actual organization—"

"Don't get carried away," Tyler interrupted. "It only takes one guy to print something like that and run it off on a photocopier."

"Come on," Sharon persisted. "The fact that these guys are coming right out and expressing their ideas means we've got a problem."

"Okay," Tyler relented. "We've got a problem."

"Are you just saying that, or do you mean it?" Sharon demanded.

She could hear the teasing note in his reply. "I mean it. But I also know better than to try and stop you once you're on a roll." Then he became more serious. "And I don't want us to get into an argument over this, okay?"

Sharon smiled. "Okay." She didn't want anything coming between them, either. But even as she changed the subject, and they began talking about other things, her eyes kept straying back to the flyer.

It was really sickening, truly horrible, that *anyone* would express ideas like this. But at least she knew now that she wouldn't have any trouble coming up with material for her show.

Five

At breakfast the next morning, Sharon regaled her parents with her thoughts on the upcoming *Video High* show. "This is going to be the most exciting show we've ever done," she promised.

"No way," her younger brother Kyle stated. "The most exciting show was the one two weeks ago."

Sharon thought back. She hadn't been involved with that particular show at all. "Which one was it?"

"The one where you had the captains of all the Greenwood teams," Kyle said. "And they told those great stories about their closest games. Now, *that* was exciting."

"Believe me, this one will be much more thrilling," Sharon declared. "Racism is a very hot issue."

"No one's talking about it in Middle School," Kyle said. He gulped down the rest of his juice. "I got basketball practice. Bye." He grabbed his books and ran out.

Mr. Delaney was eyeing Sharon curiously.

"I thought you told us last night that the show would be about race relations, not racism."

Sharon shrugged. "Race relations, racism, it's all the same thing."

"Not necessarily," her mother commented. "You're suggesting that poor race relations are due to racism. They may just be due to the fact that people haven't made the effort to get to know each other."

Sharon reached for the orange juice. "Either way, it's going to be terrific."

"What are your plans?" her father asked.

"I'm not sure yet," Sharon told him. "I just got the topic approved yesterday. But whatever we do, I know we're going to stir things up."

She poured her juice, and then added milk to her cereal. It wasn't until she'd finished that she realized both her parents were looking at her with concern in their eyes.

"What's the matter?" she asked.

"You're going to be dealing with a pretty touchy subject," her mother remarked. "I hope you're planning to give a lot of thought to your approach."

"You'd better not come on too strong," her father cautioned her.

Sharon was aghast. Her parents had always been fervent supporters of equality and human rights. "Aren't you two opposed to racism?"

"Of course we are!" her mother exclaimed.

"Absolutely!" Mr. Delaney echoed. "All I'm saying is that you'll be treading on thin ice here. You're aware of what's been going on in some high schools."

"You don't want to instigate any violent reactions," her mother said.

"Violent reactions? At Greenwood?" Sharon uttered a short laugh. "Come on, you know how apathetic the students are. That's why they need a little shaking up."

"Maybe they need to become aware of the problem," Mrs. Delaney said. "But shaking people up too hard can make them angry. Hostility doesn't open people's minds."

"But confrontation is important," Sharon insisted. "It's the only way to solve a problem."

Her father smiled fondly. "I know this means a lot to you, honey, and I'm pleased that you care so much. But I don't think you should expect to solve the problem of racism in a one-hour cable television show."

Her mother agreed. "If you don't mind a little advice, perhaps your goal should be simply to *address* the problem. And you don't want to jump into an issue like this without giving it some serious thought. Make sure you understand exactly what the problem is, first."

Sharon wasn't disturbed by her mother's lecture. Mrs. Delaney was an instructor at Emory University, and she couldn't help frequently sounding like she was teaching a class. Sharon was accustomed to her tone.

Besides, she *did* understand the problem. That flyer she'd found on her car yesterday

. made it all too painfully clear. There were some sick, disgusting people at Greenwood, and the rest of the students had to be made aware that there were enemies sitting in their classrooms.

But she didn't show the flyer to her parents. She was afraid it would upset them too much. "I'd better get to school," she told them. "Listen, don't worry about the show. Mr. Russell won't let us go wild and crazy."

She left the house, and got into her mother's old car, which had become hers when her mother bought a new one last month. Even though her mother had given her free use of it before, knowing that the car was now hers alone gave Sharon an enormous sense of independence.

And she needed to feel independent and self-reliant. She suspected that she was going to have to pretty much shoulder the responsibility of this show alone. Although people had supported her at the meeting yesterday, nobody seemed as excited about it as she was. She doubted that she'd get much serious help, even from friends like Tyler, Jade, and Debra. They were all much too cautious.

She was going to carry the show on her own, but that was okay. It might even make things easier. She'd be able to do exactly what she wanted to do, without having to seek the others' approval or battle their opposition.

However, she still didn't know exactly what

she wanted to do, how she'd approach the format. Her mind began moving faster than the car. Who should she invite to appear on the show? She recalled that a member of the school board was black. Maybe he'd be good . . . Howard Weller would be appearing on the show, so maybe he'd be part of her panel, too. There was so much to think about, so much planning to do. And she was going to love every moment of it. Here was a real opportunity to make a change in people's lives, to make their lives better.

She was on a high as she strolled into the school building. And she was still beaming when she ran into Jeff Russell, who was emerging from the assistant principal's office. "Hi!" she called out gaily.

Jeff's greeting wasn't accompanied by his usual cheery expression. "Sharon, I'm glad to see you. There's something we have to talk about."

"What's that?" Sharon asked.

"Walk with me to my room," Jeff said. As they moved through the usual crowds that gathered in the school lobby before homeroom, she looked at him worriedly. Jeff did not look happy.

He didn't speak until they reached the relative quiet of a hallway. "Mr. Quimby called me in this morning," he told her. "He heard about our topic for *Video High*. He doesn't think race relations is an appropriate subject now."

Sharon wasn't terribly dismayed. "Mr. Quimby hardly ever likes our topics. He's always saying that they're too controversial."

"I'm afraid this time he was adamant," Jeff said. "He's vetoed the show."

"But he can't do that!" Sharon exclaimed. "We have the power to run our own shows, right? He doesn't have the authority to forbid us."

"In principle, that's true," Jeff said slowly. "But he does have general authority over authorized student organizations. The only difference between *Video High* and any other group at Greenwood is the fact that we're operating under a grant, and not funded by the school." He paused. "I have to say, Sharon, that he did make some good points."

"Like what?" Sharon demanded. She couldn't imagine the cranky assistant principal ever making a good point about anything.

"As you know, race relations have been tense at several area high schools lately," Jeff said. "People are on edge. This may not be the best time to air a show on such a volatile topic."

Incredulous, Sharon gaped. "You mean, you're giving in to him?"

"It's not a question of giving in, or giving up the topic completely, either," Jeff stated.

"But we need to proceed carefully. We should rework the subject, emphasizing that it's not about racism, but about brotherhood." With a smile, he corrected himself. "And sisterhood. Is there a word that includes both? Peoplehood, maybe?"

Sharon didn't return the smile. "But when can we do the show?"

"Let's give Mr. Quimby time to cool down, and just put it on the back burner for a little while. A few months, maybe."

"I don't agree!" Sharon spoke pleadingly. "If race relations are tense *now*, then *now* is the time to talk about them."

Jeff looked sympathetic, but he shook his head. "This isn't the time to buck the assistant principal, Sharon. Our funding is coming up for renewal soon, and—"

Sharon interrupted. "But you just said that we're funded by a grant, not by the school. If the school doesn't pay for *Video High,* then Quimby can't tell us what to do."

Jeff spoke kindly, but firmly. "Let me finish. We need the school administration's support for our application to have the grant renewed."

He put a hand on her shoulder. "Sharon, I know you're disappointed. But sometimes we have to accept the fact that things can't always go the way we want them to." He glanced up at the clock. It was just about time for the bell. "I have to get to homeroom and so do you. We'll talk about this some more later, okay?"

Sharon was dragging her feet all the way to her own classroom. Inside, she was steaming. Accept it, Jeff had said. To Sharon, accepting meant giving up. It meant defeat.

She tried to understand Jeff's point of view. After all, he was employed by the school. He couldn't fight Mr. Quimby—he might lose his job. But what did Sharon have to lose? She wouldn't get suspended for trying to hold on to her show. She could do something. But what?

It was just as she walked into her home-room that an idea came to her. Maybe it was the ringing of the bell that triggered it. She strode to the teacher's desk, and spoke.

"Could I have an excuse to go to the principal's office?"

Fortunately, the teacher was so busy collating some papers that she didn't bother to ask Sharon why. With the permission slip in hand, Sharon dashed out of the room.

She was nervous as she walked into the administrative waiting room. Dr. Moorhead wasn't someone she approached every day. Few students encountered her on any regular basis. Quimby was the one who dealt with the student body. Sharon wasn't even sure exactly what the head principal did. But she knew that Dr. Moorhead was the real boss, the person in this school with the ultimate authority.

"I'd like to see Dr. Moorhead, please," she told the secretary.

The woman looked at her askance, as if Sharon had asked permission to see the President of the United States. "You want to see *Dr. Moorhead?*"

"Yes. Please."

"Do you have an appointment?"

"No."

Now, the secretary was appalled. "You can't see the principal without an appointment!"

Sharon cast aside all attempts to appear dignified. "Please," she begged. "It's urgent, and it will only take a few minutes, really, I swear." She tried to look as pathetic and needy as possible, and she must have succeeded because the secretary seemed to soften.

"Well, Dr. Moorhead is very busy," she said, stressing the word very. "But I'll see if she can squeeze you in."

She went to a door, rapped lightly, and went in. A second later, she reappeared. "Dr. Moorhead can see you for one minute," she said. "Go on in."

Sharon went into the principal's office. The gray-haired woman at the desk looked up and smiled. "Good morning," she said. "And you are . . . ?"

"Sharon Delaney, I'm a junior," Sharon replied, her voice quavering a bit.

"Have a seat, Sharon. What can I do for you?"

Sharon spoke rapidly. "I'm with *Video High*, and we want to do a show about race relations . . . um, brotherhood, getting along, that sort of thing."

Dr. Moorhead nodded slightly, indicating that she should go on.

"Well, I, um, thought we should get your permission."

"Why?" Dr. Moorhead asked. *"Video High* has dealt with a number of controversial topics. I don't recall being asked for my approval before."

Sharon squirmed slightly in her chair. "Well, some people think it's a touchy subject, because of problems at other schools and all that."

The principal raised her eyebrows. "Some people?"

"Um, Mr. Quimby, um, expressed some concern . . . but the show would have a positive attitude, you know, upbeat."

The telephone on the desk buzzed, and Dr. Moorhead picked it up. "Yes? The superintendent? Oh, put him on." Then she covered the mouthpiece with her hand and spoke hurriedly to Sharon. "I have to take this call, dear. Thank you for coming by." Into the phone, she said, "Good morning, Dr. Saunders, how nice to hear from you."

"Then it's okay?" Sharon asked eagerly. "For us to do this show?"

"One moment," the principal said into the phone, and turned to Sharon. "Yes, dear, I look forward to seeing it." Her tone was impatient and distracted, but Sharon didn't care. She had what she'd come for.

Leaving the office, she flew down the hall and went directly to Jeff Russell's homeroom. She opened the classroom door and walked right in.

He looked up, startled, and Sharon stopped suddenly. What was she doing? You didn't just walk into a room in the middle of a class period, even if it was just homeroom. She was aware of the class staring at her, and she was acutely embarrassed.

But it was too late to do anything about it, so she went to Jeff's desk and spoke to him in a whisper. "Could I see you for a minute?"

He rose and went with her out into the hall. "What's wrong, Sharon?"

She forgot her initial embarrassment and spoke happily. "Nothing's wrong, everything's right! I'm sorry I burst into your class like that, but I couldn't wait to tell you."

"Tell me what?"

She described her meeting with Dr. Moorhead. Jeff listened, and lines began to cross his forehead. The more she told him, the deeper the lines became.

He didn't look pleased, and she couldn't understand. "You see, Jeff, we can do the show now! If Dr. Moorhead says it's okay,

Quimby can't do anything about it. And we'll still have *her* support for our funding. Aren't you glad?"

For the first time ever, Jeff looked practically stern. "Sharon, did it occur to you that perhaps you should have consulted me before going to see Dr. Moorhead? I *am* the advisor of the group, and that's what I'm here for, to give advice."

"I . . . I guess I was so excited about the idea, I didn't think about that," Sharon confessed.

"You know, you could have put *Video High* in jeopardy," Jeff continued. "Dr. Moorhead might have been annoyed by the fact that you were going over Mr. Quimby's head. And keep in mind that *Video High* makes its decisions based on the group's consensus, not the decisions of one person."

Sharon felt deservedly chastised. She bit her lip. "I'm sorry. I know I should have talked to you first. I didn't consider all the possible consequences." She gave him an abashed, apologetic smile. "Sometimes I leap before I look."

After a moment, he spoke more gently. "Well, I *am* pleased that we'll be able to do the show. But next time, Sharon, think before you act."

"I will," Sharon promised.

Walking back to her own homeroom, she did accept the fact that she'd been foolish, rushing off to see the principal. But then, re-calling Jeff's expression and his words, she be-gan to feel a little annoyed. She hadn't been scolded like that by a teacher since she was a child.

He really shouldn't have come down on her that hard, she thought. Okay, maybe she *had* moved too quickly, and gone over people's heads. But in the long run, as far as *Video High* was concerned, it had all worked out to their advantage. And sometimes the ends *did* justify the means.

Debra came out of her last class and saw Jade waving to her from across the hall. She maneuvered her way through the deluge of students emerging from the rooms and joined her.

"Are you going to Harry's with Sharon and me?" Jade asked her.

"I can't," Debra replied. "I'm meeting Steve Nowicki."

"Steve Nowicki!" Jade sucked in her breath and placed a hand over her heart. "Wow, he's *hot!* When did you get together with Steve Nowicki? Tell, tell, what's the story?"

"There's no story," Debra said. "We're work-ing on a project for our English class, that's all."

"Too bad," Jade sighed. "What kind of project?"

"We have to rewrite a scene from *Romeo and Juliet.*"

"*Romeo and Juliet,* huh?" Jade's eyebrows waggled up and down. "*That* sounds promising."

"And *you* sound like Kris Hogan," Debra retorted.

Jade cringed, and then gave a shrug. "Oh, well, if you're not interested in Steve Nowicki, give him my phone number."

Debra laughed, waved, and moved on down the hall. She knew Jade was joking, but she tried to picture Jade and Steve together anyway. She decided it wouldn't work. She didn't think Steve would go for a girl with purple streaks in her hair, and she doubted that Jade would be attracted to a guy who didn't have any tattoos.

She turned the corner to the corridor lined with lockers, and noticed a small group of students clustered around a sign on the wall. Curious, she paused as she passed them, to see what had caught their attention.

It was a handmade poster, with the words written in heavy black marker. ATTENTION ALL WHITE STUDENTS it proclaimed. STAND UP FOR YOUR RACE! SHOW PRIDE IN YOUR CAUCASIAN HERITAGE! COME TO THE FIRST MEETING OF THE PRO-WHITE UNION! FRIDAY, 3:30, ROOM 228.

Debra hugged her books tighter, and tried to ignore the icy shiver that passed through her. Somehow, the poster was a lot more powerful than the flyer she'd seen yesterday. It seemed to demand a stronger reaction.

She was almost afraid to check out the reactions of the students around her. But she didn't have to look at them to learn their responses.

"Gross," someone muttered. "Who *are* these people?"

"Bunch of losers," someone else replied. "Sickos."

A girl read aloud from the poster. " 'Show pride in your Caucasian heritage.' What is that supposed to mean?"

Another girl answered. "I guess that's what you show pride in when you don't have anything else going for you. What do you think these jerks do in this meeting?"

A boy had an idea. "Maybe they're going to sit around and compare their skin to see who's the lightest."

That got some laughs, and Debra was able to smile, too. It was a relief to hear them making fun of this group.

More students had gathered around, and there were more jokes. "Why should I stand up for my race?" a guy asked. "What did my race ever do for me?"

" 'Pro-White Union,' " another boy read. "Does that mean these are professional white guys?"

"Yeah," someone else replied. "No amateurs allowed."

"What's going on here?" a harsh voice behind them bellowed.

The crowd parted, and Mr. Quimby stormed through them. He got a view of the poster. "Who's responsible for this?" he demanded to know. Without waiting for an answer, he tore the poster down and crumpled it. Then he strode away.

The crowd began to disperse. Debra lingered for a few seconds. She could still see the bits of tape that had held the poster to the wall. And even though the poster was gone, the words reverberated in her memory.

Then she remembered Steve, and she tore herself away from the blank wall.

He was waiting by her locker. "Sorry I'm late," she said breathlessly.

"No problem," he replied with a smile. "Ready to go back on the balcony?"

"Just let me get my stuff together." She twirled her combination and opened the locker. "Do you want to go back to my place to work?"

"I was thinking, maybe we should go to the public library," Steve suggested. "It might be helpful to look at some books about interpreting Shakespeare."

Debra was impressed. That idea hadn't even occurred to her. And how many boys at Greenwood High would even know that such books existed?

Approaching his car, she felt her heart

quicken, and realized she was staring straight at the windshield. But there was no flyer on it today. That was a relief. But she wished she could stop thinking about that sign.

"Did you see that poster?" Steve asked as they pulled out of the parking lot.

She considered asking "what poster," but that was silly. "Yes."

"Pretty nauseating, huh?"

"Mm. Kids were laughing at it."

"I don't know if it's a laughing matter," Steve said.

Debra did not want to get into a discussion of this. "I was glad to hear Mr. Russell say we don't have to memorize our lines, weren't you?"

He took his eyes off the road just long enough to give her a brief, appraising look. Then he said, "Yeah, it's going to make this presentation a lot easier."

She relaxed. He must have sensed her reluctance to talk about the poster. What a nice guy, she thought.

At the public library, they checked the catalog and located a book called *Romeo and Juliet: Critical and Interpretive Essays*. They settled down at a table with it, and explored the table of contents together.

After a moment, they exchanged the same expressions of distaste.

"Does this make sense to you?" Debra asked.

"I can't even tell what these chapters are about," Steve said.

"Let's look at one of the essays," Debra said. She picked one at random and flipped the pages. Huddled close together, they began to read. Before long, they were looking at each other in despair.

"This interpretation is harder to understand than Shakespeare," Steve declared.

From behind them, a voice declared, "Well, you two look chummy."

They both turned to see Tracy Egan, a classmate, standing there with a teasing smile on her face. She was clutching a copy of *Hamlet*. "Which play are you two working on?" she asked.

"*Romeo and Juliet*," Debra told her.

"Lucky you," Tracy commented.

"Why?" Steve asked.

"All you two have to do is fall madly in love." Tracy made a face. "I'm Ophelia in *Hamlet*. I have to go insane."

"Same difference," Steve said with a grin. "Going crazy, falling in love . . ."

"That's a good point," Tracy agreed, laughing. "Here comes my Hamlet."

Debra saw Carl Perez coming toward them. Privately, she thought it was too bad the assignments weren't reversed, that Carl and Tracy hadn't been given the *Romeo and Juliet* scene. They'd been going together for ages. As for herself, she doubted faking insanity was that much more difficult than faking passion. She wondered which part Steve would prefer—the lovesick Romeo or the brooding Prince of Denmark?

Tracy and Carl joined them at their table, and Steve showed them the book of essays they'd found. They, too, found it impossible to read.

"Russell says we should try to understand the motives of our characters," Carl said. He scowled. "Personally, I don't get this guy Hamlet."

"Think about how you'd feel if you suspected your uncle of killing your father," Debra suggested. "And then your mother marries your uncle, the murderer! Wouldn't that make you pretty depressed?"

"I don't have an uncle," Carl sighed. He turned to Steve. "Do you have a handle on Romeo?"

"Sort of," Steve admitted. "He's in love with this girl, both their families are against it, and practically the whole world's trying to split them up. I think I can imagine what that would be like."

"You've got a better imagination than I have," Carl grumbled. He opened his book. "What does this mean?" he asked, pointing to a passage.

The four of them started discussing their scenes, going over lines and offering each other advice. After about an hour, they were all wiped out.

"Thanks for the help," Carl told Steve. "I got way behind in the fall, because of football practice, and it's not easy catching up."

Debra remembered that Carl was the captain of Greenwood's football team. "You must be glad the football season's over," Debra commented.

"*I* certainly am," Tracy said. "I hardly ever saw him out of a helmet."

"Yeah, it's good watching other guys knock themselves out for a change," Carl said. "The basketball team's doing pretty good this year. A bunch of us are going to the game Friday. You guys want to come?"

"Sounds good to me," Steve said, and turned to Debra. "How about it?"

Debra didn't have any other plans for Friday night. "All right."

Carl and Tracy started off, but after a few seconds, Tracy came hurrying back. "I hope Carl didn't put you guys on the spot," she said. "Sometimes he doesn't think."

"What do you mean?" Debra asked.

"Well, you don't *have* to hang out at the game with us. If you want to be alone, I understand." She smiled wistfully. "I remember how Carl and I felt, at the beginning. We could never get enough time alone."

Debra stared at her, speechless.

"It's okay," Steve told Tracy.

She smiled brightly at them. "Great. See you tomorrow in class."

She thinks we're a couple, Debra thought as she watched Tracy hurry away. Why couldn't people accept that a boy and a girl could be friends?

She noticed that Steve was staring after Tracy, too. Suddenly, she was very embarrassed by this. But once again, Steve understood her feelings.

He looked at her, winked, and grinned. She grinned back. And any tension disappeared when they both burst out laughing.

Six

Sitting in his last class on Friday afternoon, Zack kept taking peeks at his watch. In just fifteen minutes, he could escape this place. Never before had he looked forward so much to a weekend, despite the fact that he had nothing special planned for it. But it was two whole days in which he could hide from his classmates, from their pity and their scorn.

Stop exaggerating, he berated himself. It's all in your head. Not that many kids have been giving you those mocking looks. One or two guys, maybe, and they're just people who used to be jealous of you.

Used to be. That was the key phrase. Sure, those guys were jealous, back when he was president of his class, when students sucked up to him, and even administrators like Mr. Quimby treated him with respect. He couldn't imagine that anyone envied him *now.* Nobody paid any attention to him *now.* He was just another student, a nobody.

That was what really bothered him. Not the occasional expression of dislike or disdain. It was the total neglect, it was being completely ignored.

He tried to think up some plans for the weekend, something to do that might lift his spirits. He could go to the country club, and hang out with the private school guys. But maybe that wasn't such a good idea. His father had surely bragged to his cronies that his son was destined to be *Metro Magazine*'s Outstanding Senior. The men had probably told their sons. *They'd* be the ones who'd really look down on him.

So he'd spend the weekend just like he'd spent every evening since Monday—in his room, emerging only for meals. And the meals were something to dread. He'd be in the same room as his father, and he'd feel his father's contempt. Maybe he could plead a headache, a stomachache, the flu. . . . No, that would only make things worse. His father viewed all illnesses as just another form of personal weakness.

The sound of his own name penetrated the gloom of his thoughts. He looked up.

The teacher's voice was sarcastic. "Would you care to join the class, mentally as well as physically?"

The other students tittered. Zack felt like sinking under his desk. Now they were actually laughing at him.

The bell rang, and Zack pretended to be busy searching for something in the storage area under his chair. On the one hand, he couldn't get out of this room, this building, fast enough. But the longer he waited to emerge from the classroom, the less possibility there was to run into anyone.

He was the last to rise from his desk. But when he reached the door, he found Brett there, blocking his departure. He fought off a desire to brutally shove him out of his way.

Brett wore that dopey, puppy-dog, pathetic smile. "Hi, I was waiting for you!"

"What do you want?" Zack asked rudely.

His attitude didn't seem to bother Brett at all. "I thought you might want to check out this meeting."

"What meeting?"

"Didn't you see the poster?" Brett asked.

Zack was about to lose what little patience he had. *"What* poster?"

Brett explained. "There's a meeting of something called the Pro-White Union. I saw the announcement Wednesday. The poster's gone now, but I guess the meeting's still on."

"I don't even know what this Pro-White Union is," Zack snapped.

"Neither do I," Brett told him. He described what the poster had said.

"They sound like cranks," Zack muttered.

"It might be interesting," Brett said. "At least we know it's exclusive." He smirked meaningfully. "It's a pretty safe bet that Howard Weller won't be there."

He must have noticed that Zack didn't look convinced, because he began wheedling. "Aw, come on, it'll be good for a laugh if nothing else."

Zack thought he could use a laugh right about now, though he doubted very much that this Pro-White thing would provide it. But he was curious, he couldn't deny it. So he shrugged, and nodded, and they took off down the hall.

He allowed Brett to lead him upstairs, to room 228. Through the door's window, Zack counted eight students, all male. Several had shaved heads. They didn't look like Zack's kind of people or his kind of scene.

But Brett had already opened the door, and several heads had turned to see who was coming in. He'd look foolish if he turned away.

They took seats in the back of the classroom. One of the boys looked vaguely familiar, and Zack recalled him being in one of his classes. His name was Kurt something, Zack thought. Rhodes, Kurt Rhodes.

When he got a good look at another guy, he groaned silently. Denny Banks. A real moron. The kind of guy who walked around with a spray paint can in his back pocket, just in case he saw a wall that didn't have any graffiti on it.

Denny had recognized him, too. He was clearly surprised to see Zack there.

At least Denny didn't appear to be the

leader here. Another boy, someone Zack didn't know, got up and addressed the group. "Uh, I'm Todd Granger, and I guess we should get started."

Before he could go any further, a nervous-looking dweeb said, "Maybe you should wait till more people get here."

"I don't think we're going to get any more," another boy said. "The posters got torn down. We got ten here, that's enough."

"What's the big deal, we can wait five more minutes," someone else declared.

As they all began to bicker over whether to start or wait, Zack took the opportunity to get a good look at this Todd Granger. He seemed awfully young, maybe just a sophomore, not old enough to shave.

At least he wasn't bald, like some of the guys. And he was dressed decently, too, in khakis and a sweater and normal shoes, not those huge black lace-up boots some of the others were wearing. He made Zack think that maybe not all these characters were major nerds.

But he didn't seem to have much control over this group. They were still squabbling, and Zack turned to Brett in disgust. "I'm getting out of here."

"Wait a minute," Todd called out as Zack rose. "Hang around, we *are* going to have a meeting."

"When?" Zack asked belligerently.

"Right now," Todd replied, his anxious eyes darting among the others. "I'm calling to order this, uh, first meeting of the Pro-White Union. Most of us know each other." He looked at the back of the room. "You guys want to introduce yourselves?"

"Brett Calhoun."

"Zack Stevenson. Look, what is this group for? What's your mission?"

Todd considered the question. "We want to, you know, get white people united."

"United for what?" Zack asked. "To do what?"

Kurt Rhodes jumped in. "To fight back. So we won't get pushed around anymore. Minority groups are taking over, in case you haven't noticed. Now *we're* the ones who are deprived."

"Yeah," Denny Banks blurted out. "Minorities get all the breaks. White guys are getting a raw deal."

Another skinhead spoke up. "It's time to show people that in this country, the majority still rules!" This was punctuated by a cheer from the others.

When the noise died down, Zack asked, "Exactly how are you going to do this?"

"We don't know, *yet*," Todd said. "That's why we're forming this group. So we can make some plans. We have to let people know what's going on."

"Right, we gotta stir things up," Denny exclaimed.

Another boy began ranting about how some black guy beat him out for a job bagging groceries at a supermarket, and others joined in with grievances. In Zack's opinion, they sounded like a bunch of whining babies.

"What do you think of this?" Brett asked Zack softly.

Zack leaned forward. "Wimps," he whispered back. "They don't know what they're doing. They're totally disorganized."

"Yeah, but they're on the right track," Brett replied. "I mean, they got the right ideas. And a disorganized group like this, they're ripe for a takeover. All they need is a leader." He paused, and then added, "Someone like you."

Zack frowned slightly, and sat back. He hadn't even considered that possibility. Brett had a point. This group needed a leader, someone to speak for them, someone who could present a good image. Todd was the only one who looked okay, but he didn't have leadership qualities.

Did he himself have leadership qualities? His father certainly didn't think so. Maybe . . . maybe there was a possibility here of proving him wrong.

But would he even want to take over a ragged group of losers like this? Could he shape them into something credible, a group with some power?

As he pondered this, the door to the classroom opened and Mr. Quimby walked in. "What's going on here?" he demanded.

Todd began to stammer. "We're, we're, uh, having a meeting. Sir."

"Who's having a meeting? What organization is this?"

One of the skinheads rose and spoke. "We're the Pro-White Union." The unspoken words, "and what are you going to do about it," hung in the air like a silent challenge.

Mr. Quimby faced them grimly. "You are *not* an authorized Greenwood High School organization."

"So what?" Kurt asked.

The assistant principal's face turned crimson. "So what? So that means you have no business being here, you have no right to meet on school property. I'm ordering you to vacate these premises immediately."

A couple of guys began to get up and gather their coats, but Zack found Quimby's attitude to be very annoying. He rose. "Excuse me, Mr. Quimby, but all these people are students at Greenwood. Doesn't that give them the right to be here? Is there a rule that says they have to be out of the building by a certain time?"

Mr. Quimby eyed him irritably. "They don't have the right to hold a meeting if they're not recognized as an official activity. And what are *you* doing here?"

"I'm an interested observer," Zack replied smoothly. "Mr. Quimby, doesn't the Constitution of the United States guarantee citizens the right of assembly?"

"We have our own rules," Mr. Quimby barked. "This group is not recognized."

"Then how do they *get* recognized?" Zack asked.

Quimby's eyes narrowed. "What *is* this Pro-White Union anyway?"

"It's a club for white people," Denny yelled.

"Only white people?" Quimby asked.

There was a chorus of "yeahs."

Quimby responded with a thin, triumphant smile. "Then it's discriminatory. We don't allow groups that discriminate to meet on school grounds. You *can't* be recognized."

Zack had expected to hear an argument like that from Quimby, and he was prepared with a response. "What about the African American Students League? Only black students are members of that. Why are they allowed to meet on school property and we can't?" With a start, he realized that he had said "we," not "they." Was he beginning to think of himself as more than just an interested observer?

"That's entirely different!" the assistant principal declared hotly.

"How?"

"They're *recognized!*"

Zack wasn't finished. "Did you ever hear of freedom of speech? Don't we have the right to express our views?"

"Not on school grounds!" Quimby bellowed.

"You people have five minutes to be out of here. And I'll be back to make sure you're gone!" With that, he left the room.

For a second or two, the room was silent. And then Todd said, "That was cool, Stevenson."

"Yeah," Kurt agreed. "You really told him off."

"We still have to get out of here," Denny pointed out.

"Right," another guy said, "but Stevenson put up a good fight. He really defended us."

Kurt ambled back to where Zack was still standing. "I used to think you were a pretty stuck-up guy, a regular preppie snob. But I guess I had you figured wrong."

They were all gathering around him now, shaking his hand, speaking words of appreciation. Brett was smiling at him, and looking proud.

Zack listened to their words appreciatively, and he took even more pleasure at their expressions. They were looking at him with respect, and admiration. He hadn't seen looks like this for a long time.

It felt nice. The dark clouds that had been surrounding him began to lift. And suddenly, these guys didn't seem like such losers anymore.

"Debra," Mrs. Lewis called. "Sharon's here."

Debra pulled on a bathrobe and hurried out to the living room. "Hi, what are you doing here?"

"I was driving down the street," Sharon said. "I'm meeting Tyler at the movies in half an hour and I'm early, so I thought I'd stop by here. Are you sick?"

"No, why?"

"What are you doing in your bathrobe at seven o'clock?"

"I just got out of the shower," Debra said. "I'm going out in a little while. C'mon back to my room, I have to get ready."

"You've got a *date*?!" Sharon's face was a combination of astonishment and glee.

"No, I don't have a date. I'm going to the basketball game at school."

"You're going to the *basketball game*?" Now, only the astonishment remained.

Debra wasn't surprised by Sharon's reaction. Not only had Debra never been to a basketball game before, she'd never shown the most remote interest in going. High school sports had never been high on her list of things to do for fun.

"I'm trying to be open-minded," Debra explained. "It's healthy to expose one's self to new experiences." She sat down at her vanity table and began braiding her hair.

"Who are you going with?" Sharon asked, plopping down on Debra's bed.

"Tracy Egan, Carl Perez, and Steve

Nowicki." She told Sharon about running into Tracy and Carl at the public library, and their invitation to her and Steve. "And then, Tracy came running back to tell us she'd understand if Steve and I preferred to be alone." She laughed. "Can you believe that? She thought we'd been dating!"

"Why do you think it's so funny?" Sharon asked. "I can understand why she'd think that. After all, you've been getting together with him practically every day after school this week. Beth Ann told me she saw y'all at Harry's. And you two had your heads together in the cafeteria yesterday and today. . . . What else are people going to think?"

"Oh, for crying out loud," Debra murmured. "Can't a girl and a boy work on homework together and be friends without people thinking they're *involved?*"

"Well, he's awfully cute . . ." Sharon got up and went to Debra's closet. "What are you going to wear?"

"I don't know, some old thing," Debra said carelessly. "What do people wear to basketball games anyway? Jeans?"

Sharon nodded, and selected a white silk shirt to go with them.

"I'll freeze in that," Debra objected, and put on a dark red turtleneck. Then Sharon rummaged through Debra's jewelry box, and picked out some long glittery earrings.

"No, those are too fussy," Debra said, and

chose some tiny gold studs instead. Fully dressed, she presented herself for inspection.

Sharon eyed her critically. "Have you ever tried eyeliner? It would make your eyes look bigger."

Debra picked up her glasses. "What's the point? No one can see my eyes behind these."

"You're going to wear your *glasses?*" Sharon yelped.

"It might help me to understand the game if I can see it," Debra replied.

"You're hopeless," Sharon moaned. "Jazz yourself up a little! You don't want to look the same way you look at school." She burrowed through Debra's closet and emerged with a long scarf. "Wear this."

Debra fingered the silk thoughtfully. "How many years does a person get jailed for strangling her best friend?"

She *did* allow herself a little spritz of perfume, and then, thankfully, Sharon had to leave. A short time later, Debra was leaving the house herself, with Steve.

"Your parents are terrific," Steve told her.

"I told you they were cool," Debra said. "Didn't you believe me?"

"They made me feel so welcome," Steve marveled.

"Of course they did," Debra replied. "They make all my friends feel welcome." Her eyes twinkled as she teased, "Even the white ones."

Greenwood's basketball team was having a

winning season, so the gym was crowded, with Greenwood students on one side and Weston students on the other. They found Tracy and Carl on the bleachers, and Debra was amused by the way Tracy made Carl move closer so Debra and Steve could sit together.

Carl was enthused about the game they were about to see. "This will be a close match," he told Debra. "It ought to be exciting."

"I've never been to a basketball game before," Debra confessed.

Both Steve and Carl began explaining the rules to her. But before they could get very far, Tracy clutched Carl's arm. "Uh-oh, here comes Caroline Dean," she said. She maneuvered Carl's arm around her shoulder.

Debra was only slightly familiar with the girl who was climbing the bleachers and coming toward them. She seemed to be eyeing them all keenly as she greeted them, but she focused particularly on Debra. "You're Debra Lewis, right?"

Debra nodded. "We were in the same Spanish class last year."

As soon as Caroline moved on, Tracy released Carl's arm. "I always make him do that when we see Caroline," she confided in Debra. "A couple of months ago, we ran into her at the movies, and we weren't even holding hands. You can imagine what she did about that."

Debra didn't have the slightest idea what

Tracy was talking about, and her expression made that clear.

"Caroline writes the gossip column for the Greenwood *News*," Tracy explained. "After she saw Carl and me standing apart in the lobby of the movie theater, the next week her column reported that our relationship seemed to be falling apart."

A roar went up from both sides of the gym, indicating that the players had come onto the floor. As the game began, Debra watched in bewilderment. Guys raced up and down the court, bouncing the ball and throwing it so fast she couldn't even figure out which team had it. It was like watching a movie video on fast forward. And the score kept changing so rapidly, it was impossible to keep track of who was ahead. Every time she tore her eyes away from the court to look at the score board, it had changed.

Steve tried to explain what was going on to her. When two players collided, a whistle blew, and the game stopped. "What happened?" Debra asked.

"One of their guys ran into one of ours," Steve told her. "The referee is calling a foul. Now, watch, the coach is arguing with him. Sometimes, it's hard to tell if what happened was an accident or intentional."

The referee's decision prevailed, and the game continued. But then, there was another run-in between players—which looked to Debra like one guy was shoving another. The guy who had been shoved fell down, and the whistle blew again.

"That was no accident!" Carl exclaimed.

It was clear that the guy who had fallen didn't think so, either. He got up and shoved the player who'd pushed him.

"Is he supposed to do that?" Debra asked innocently.

Obviously, not. Suddenly, there was a fight going on between the two guys. Several more players gathered around. The crowd went crazy, screaming and yelling. The referee broke up the fight, and the guys involved were ejected from the floor.

Wide-eyed, Debra turned to Steve. "Does that happen a lot?"

"Sometimes things can get a little crazy," Steve admitted. "People become upset, especially when one team disagrees with a referee's call." He looked distinctly troubled. "I hope that's all it was about."

"What do you mean?" Debra asked.

"Didn't you notice?" Steve asked. "The Weston player was black, ours was white."

Debra was floored. "You think it was a *racial* thing?"

Carl had been listening, and he broke in. "Could have been. Most of the Weston players are black, most of ours are white. Some of the Greenwood guys might have just been looking for an excuse to start something. These things happen . . ."

Tracy jumped in with her opinion. "I think it was just an argument over the ruling, that's all."

"I agree," Debra said quickly.

But the incident kept her from really enjoying the rest of the game. She was beginning to wonder if there were more tensions at Greenwood than she thought. She started watching the game carefully, and every time a black player and a white player went after the ball, she tensed up.

Even when Greenwood won, she found it hard to join in the cheering. "We're going to Harry's," Carl told Steve. "You guys want to come?"

Steve turned to Debra, who nodded. "I've got my car, we'll meet you there," Steve told them.

Out in the parking lot, Debra said, "You don't *really* think the fight was a racial thing, do you? I mean, it might just have been a coincidence, that one guy was white and the other black. Right?"

"That's possible," Steve said, but he didn't look convinced. They had reached his car when he stopped short. "What's the matter?" Debra asked, and then she saw it, too. A piece of paper, stuck in the windshield.

Steve took it off and read it. Even under

the dim lights of the parking lot, Debra could see his face darken.

"What is it?" she asked.

"It's nothing," he said quietly, but Debra took it out of his hand.

She read the scrawled note aloud. " 'Nowicki, you're a disgrace to all white people. What's the matter with you? Can't you find a decent white girl to date? You embarrass the entire Aryan race when you go out with a dirty—' " She stopped right there and caught her breath.

That last word—it was like a knife, puncturing her voice. It was the nastiest, most derogatory expression ever applied to people of African descent. She couldn't bring herself to say it out loud. It was a word she'd heard said by racist characters in movies, but never, never in real life.

She was barely aware of Steve taking the note out of her hand. Her head was spinning. Finally, she managed to formulate a question. "Was—was there a signature?"

"No, not really. It was signed 'Pro-White Union.' "

"But it had to be someone here at Greenwood," Debra whispered. "Whoever wrote it knew your name, knew which car was yours. Maybe they saw us coming out of it when we arrived."

Steve didn't say anything. He was busily tearing the paper, shredding it into tiny pieces.

Debra heard footsteps behind her, and she

whirled around. But it was just a couple of students who barely glanced at them as they walked on by.

Was this how she would always feel now, every time she saw a classmate? Would she be wondering, "Did you write that note? Did you call me that terrible word?"

She became aware of Steve gazing at her worriedly. "Are you all right?"

She swallowed with difficulty. "Yes. But, Steve . . . I don't want to go to Harry's, okay?"

She expected him to agree. To her surprise, he said, "We have to go there, Debra."

"Why? Tracy and Carl won't mind . . ."

He shook his head, and spoke grimly. "That's not the point. Don't you see, Debra? If we don't go to Harry's like we planned to do, we're giving in to these racist thugs. We're allowing them to scare us off, we're letting them believe we care what they think of us. If we don't go to Harry's, and walk in together . . . then they've won. Do you see what I mean?"

She did. She couldn't say she was much in the mood for crowded, noisy Harry's, but Steve was right.

"Okay," she said. As they drove to Harry's, she concentrated on steeling herself for her entrance with Steve. What if whoever wrote this note was there, watching them?

She glanced at Steve. He had paused at a

stop sign, and gave her a reassuring smile. She began to relax.

At least she wouldn't be facing this alone.

Seven

On Monday afternoon in the cafeteria, Debra walked toward the table where Sharon and Jade were eating. Balancing her tray and her books, she paused. "Hi, guys," she said.

Sharon made a welcoming gesture toward the empty chair next to her, but Debra shook her head. "I have to work on this English assignment with Steve."

"You're *always* working," Sharon said. "I'll bet now you're going to say you can't go to Lenox Square with us after school today, either."

"Can you blame her?" Jade asked. "Personally, I'd rather play Romeo and Juliet with Steve Nowicki than hang at the mall with my girlfriends."

"Steve and I are not *playing* Romeo and Juliet," Debra informed her.

Jade grinned. "You mean, it's for real?"

Debra let out a heartfelt groan. Were her friends never going to let up on her? "Look, I'll meet you at my locker after school and let you know if I can go to the mall, okay? Why do you need to go there anyway?"

"I need something new to wear for the *Video High* taping Thursday," Sharon announced.

"How's that going?" Debra asked her.

"Not bad," Sharon said. "I'll tell you about it after school."

Debra was about to move on when she noticed a copy of the Greenwood High *News* lying on Sharon's stack of books. "Have you read that yet?"

"No, why?"

"I just wondered if there was anything interesting in it."

"In the *News?*" Sharon and Jade spoke in unison, and they looked equally incredulous.

"Never mind," Debra said hastily. "See y'all later."

What she'd wanted to know was whether there was any report about the fight at Friday's basketball game. She hadn't heard any discussion of it that morning. There was a boy in one of her classes who was on the team, and she'd considered asking him if he knew what the fight had really been about. But she hadn't. Maybe because she didn't really want to know.

She took a seat in the back of the cafeteria, where she knew Steve would be looking for her. With one hand, she opened her copy of *Romeo and Juliet*, and with the other, she lifted her fork.

But she didn't read, nor did she eat. She found herself gazing around the cafeteria, her eyes drifting from one noisy group to another. All she saw were nice, ordinary people, her classmates, some of whom she'd known for years. None of them looked like the kind of person who would write a disgusting note and leave it on a windshield.

But way over on the other side of the room, she did see someone who could. Actually, there were two of them—skinheads, the guys Sharon was always warning about. With their shaved heads and heavy laced-up black boots, there was something forbidding about them.

But strangely enough, seeing them here in the cafeteria didn't make her feel threatened. If anything, they looked dumb, out of place, two weirdos in a sea of normal people. There was something almost funny about them . . .

"What are you smiling about?" Steve sat down next to her.

"I was looking at those skinheads over there," she said. "And I was thinking . . . I shouldn't be so upset over one stupid note, or a flyer, or a poster. Any idiot can pull something like that together. It's not like those guys have any power."

"But they're organizing," Steve pointed out. "They've got this Pro-White Union, and they're soliciting members. I saw Zack Stevenson with them this morning!"

"Zack Stevenson's a jerk," Debra said.

"Yeah, but I would never have thought he was a racist. If those guys can start attracting people like that, they could become powerful."

"Are you trying to scare me?" Debra asked.

"No, I just think we should be realistic. These guys *can* be dangerous if they get enough followers. We have to be prepared for this, we have to fight them, we have to—"

"We have to perform *Romeo and Juliet*," Debra interrupted. "Tomorrow." She opened her book. "I rewrote this passage. It's the famous 'Romeo, Romeo, wherefore art thou' passage."

"What did you change it to?"

Debra read from her notes. "Romeo, forget about your family. If you can't do that, just tell me you love me, and I'll give up my family."

"Oh, you two are still at it!"

Both their heads shot up. Kris Hogan stood there, beaming at them.

Steve gazed at her quizzically. "We're doing an assignment, Kris."

"I know that." Kris giggled. "Everyone knows that. But it's not all work, is it?"

"What are you talking about?" Debra asked.

"Haven't you seen the *News*?" Kris opened the copy in her hands. "Right here, in the gossip column, 'Caroline's Corner.' Listen." She read aloud. " 'What two juniors, initials SN and DL, are playing Romeo and Juliet— and not just in Mr. Russell's English class! Hint—think ebony and ivory.' "

124   *Marilyn Kaye*

"Oh, no," Debra breathed.

"Caroline Dean saw you guys in the library last week," Kris reported. "Then she saw you two together at the basketball game. She put two and two together, and presto!"

Debra wanted to sink under the table. How many other kids, right that minute, were reading this little item and thinking that she and Steve were—were—a couple!

She gave him an apologetic look. To her utter amazement, he was smiling!

"You can keep this," Kris said grandly, placing the newspaper on the table. Then she whispered in Debra's ear. "You two really do make a cute couple."

She skipped off. Debra glared at Steve. "Quit grinning," she hissed. But he wouldn't. And she finally had to smile, too.

Okay, the gossip was stupid, and definitely not true. But it was kind of nice to be thought of as someone who *could* have a boyfriend.

Sharon was conducting a spontaneous interview. It was the last class of the day, and the teacher had left the room with instructions that they could talk quietly among themselves. Sharon had seized the opportunity to corner David Philby, president of the African American Students League.

She began by thanking him for agreeing to be on *Video High*. "I think it's going to be one of the most important shows we've ever done," she told him.

David agreed. "It's definitely important, and I'm glad to be a part of it. Race relations can only get better when people express and share their thoughts."

"Absolutely," Sharon said. "I'm going to work up some questions to ask you on the air. Is there anything in particular you want to talk about?"

"Well, with all the tensions at other schools, I think we should concentrate on how we can keep any conflict from coming up at Greenwood."

"But don't you think things are already tense here?" Sharon asked.

David considered this. "Not really. We get along pretty well here. But I know there are resentments and hostilities that people keep inside. And we *are* pretty divided, socially, as a school community."

"How do you feel about the skinheads, and this Pro-White Union?" Sharon asked.

David brushed that aside. "They're a handful of wackos; I'm not concerned about them. I care more about the regular kids here, who don't hate anyone—they just haven't been open to accepting each other."

"Do you think an organization like the African American Students League only encourages division?"

"No," David said. "Every minority group

has its own special problems and concerns that they need to identify together. But that doesn't mean we can't *all* come together, and make an effort to understand each other. In fact, we've been talking about this a lot lately at our meetings."

"What *is* the mission of the African American Students League?" Sharon asked.

"One of our priorities is to start having open dialogues, so that blacks and whites can learn more about each other. Asians and Hispanics, too. We need to air our feelings, and we want to improve communication between all the races. I think most students here would be open to that."

"I thought your highest priority would be to stop racism," Sharon commented. "Aren't you planning to confront this Pro-White Union?"

David smiled. "I don't think they're worth the energy. Confrontation is necessary when people are being deprived of civil rights, or when they're experiencing injustice and discrimination. But that's not what's happening here. We're more concerned with getting people to *connect*. If people get to know and appreciate others, hate-mongers can't get very far. That's the way to stop racism."

He spoke calmly and earnestly, and he sounded terribly mature for a high school junior. He obviously had put a lot of thought into this. And Sharon knew that what he was saying was true, and meaningful.

But at the same time, she was aware of feeling a twinge of disappointment. These kinds of words weren't going to get an audience worked up. David Philby wasn't going to be the most exciting panelist on her show.

Later, leaving class, she wondered who *would* be. Howard Weller was articulate, and he had a warm, appealing, easygoing personality. That's what made him so popular. He wouldn't be stirring things up. The black school board member she'd contacted was pleasant and soft spoken, a low-key woman who was mainly interested in equal educational opportunities for all young people. This wasn't adding up to drama.

Still, it would be a good show, she assured herself stoutly. It would be intelligent. But it wouldn't amaze, it wouldn't shock anyone . . .

Jade joined her in the hallway and they walked toward the lockers together. "What's really going on between Debra and Steve?" Jade asked. "She keeps denying there's anything serious, but I wonder."

"It's hard to say," Sharon replied. "Debra keeps a lot to herself. She doesn't act like she's madly in love. But she's never been involved with a guy before, so I don't know how she would react if she cared about someone."

"Maybe she's scared of relationships," Jade

remarked. "Maybe that's why she's holding back."

"It's possible," Sharon admitted. She grinned. "We'll have to give her some encouragement."

Jade nodded. "Yeah, just a little push in the right direction."

They ran into their intended victim as they turned the corner. "Hi, are you going to the mall with us?" Sharon asked.

"I wish I could," Debra told them. "But Steve and I absolutely have to go over this presentation. I'm sorry."

"That's okay," Sharon told her. "I know you'd rather be with Steve."

Debra rolled her eyes, but Sharon was pleased to note she didn't make a grand protest.

"There's something on your locker," Jade told Debra. A folded paper had been stuck there with a piece of tape.

"It might be from Steve," Debra said. "He's supposed to meet me here." She pulled off the note and opened it.

"What's the matter?" Jade asked. "Bad news?"

Debra was staring at the note, and her face had taken on a tense, strained look.

"Isn't Steve coming?" Sharon asked.

"It's not from Steve," Debra replied flatly. She didn't offer the note to Sharon, but she didn't resist when Sharon took it from her.

Sharon read it quickly. Then she read it again. "This is unbelievable."

"Let me see," Jade demanded. Sharon handed it to her, and Jade read it. For once, she was speechless.

Sharon was torn between feelings of anger at whoever wrote the note and sympathy for her best friend. "Oh, Deb. That's so disgusting. What kind of a person could write a filthy note like that?"

"It's from the Pro-White Union," Debra told her. "Steve had a note last Friday on his car."

Jade had recovered her voice. "Sick, slimy, racist pigs. This is positively nauseating." She began to read aloud. " 'Keep away from white boys, you—' " She stopped. "I can't say that word."

Sharon couldn't contain her fury. How dare anyone call her friend, or any person, such a foul name? "We have to do something about them," she raged. "They can't be allowed to get away with this."

She was floored when Debra responded mildly. "Sticks and stones can break my bones, but names will never harm me. It's not like they're actually making a threat, Sharon."

"How can you be so calm?" Sharon asked in disbelief.

"I'm trying to be rational," Debra said. "Look, they're just hateful morons, and this is how they get their kicks. They want attention. So the best thing we can do is ignore them."

"I don't agree," Sharon declared hotly. "The best thing we can do is stand up to them. *Show* them how stupid they are, and *show* them how no one cares what they say." And then an idea came to her. "Debra, they're saying black and white people shouldn't mix. Well, I want you and Steve to appear on *Video High* Thursday. As a couple."

"Are you nuts?" Debra inquired. "No way."

"Why not?"

"You know how I feel about being on television. Just thinking about it makes me feel almost as sick as reading that note. I've never appeared on camera and I never will."

"But it's for a good cause," Sharon pressed. "You can show those racists that they can't stop you."

"Stop me from what?" Debra asked.

"From being with the boy you love! You'll show them they can't break up your relationship."

"*What* relationship? Sharon, I'm not in love with Steve and he's not in love with me. I've told you, again and again, we're just friends!"

Jade jumped in. "Are you sure about that? How do you really know what Steve feels?"

Debra clutched her head. "You're giving me a headache, both of you."

"Okay," Sharon said, "maybe you two don't have a commitment. But those Pro-White people think you're dating. If you went on the show, you'd be making a statement. You owe this to others who might be involved in an interracial relationship."

"Cool it, Sharon," Jade said. "Don't try to make her feel responsible for everyone's happiness."

Sharon fell silent. She knew she was putting pressure on Debra, all in the hope of making a dramatic show. She wasn't being fair to Debra at all. "I'm sorry, Deb. I don't mean to lay a guilt trip on you."

Debra smiled wanly. "That's okay. Just don't ask me to be on the show again, okay?"

"What's going on?" Steve appeared behind Debra. Then he saw what Debra was holding, and his face darkened. "Did you get a note?"

She nodded, and handed it to him.

"I got another one, too," he said. He read Debra's note, and grimaced. "What a bunch of cowards. I wish one of them had the guts to say this to my face." His hand formed a fist, so tightly the knuckles turned white.

"Fighting doesn't solve anything," Debra said.

"Well, there are a few things I wouldn't mind saying to them," Steve muttered.

Sharon brightened. "You want an opportunity to tell these creeps exactly what you think

of them?'' When Steve nodded, she said,
"Come on *Video High* Thursday. Let everyone
know about these sleazy notes."

"You know, that's not a bad idea," Steve
said thoughtfully. Then he turned to Debra.
"We should both be on the show, together."

"Oh, Steve, no," Debra moaned.

Sharon glanced back and forth between
them. Then, abruptly, she turned to Jade.
"C'mon, I want to get to the mall. Let me
know what you decide, Steve, okay? See you
later, Deb."

"I'm surprised at you," Jade said to Sharon
once they were out of hearing distance. "Didn't
you want to stick around and try to talk her
into it?"

"No, I'm going to let Steve do that for me,"
Sharon said smugly. She turned and looked
back at them. Debra was leaning against her
locker. Steve had rested his arm on the locker
next to hers, and he was talking to her intently. Debra looked like she was listening
pretty intently, too.

Sharon smiled happily. Not only would this
be good for the show—it would be good for
Debra, too. Watching them, she had a feeling
that Debra had underestimated Steve's attitude toward her. It seemed to her that he
wanted to be more than friends. And if Debra
could get over her inhibitions, she just might
realize she felt the same.

They did make an awfully cute couple . . .

* * *

Zack parked his car on the unfamiliar street, got out, and looked around anxiously. It was a pretty sleazy neighborhood. He walked up the street and paused before a run-down diner. He pulled the note out of his pocket to see if he had the right address.

It checked out. This was where the Pro-White Union was meeting. At least he wouldn't have to worry about running into anyone he knew in a place like this.

He went in and scanned the dimly lit and dingy space. He spotted Brett and some other guys squeezed into a booth in the back. Todd saw him, and waved.

Kurt was there, too, and Denny, and another skinhead Zack didn't recognize. There was no space left in the booth.

"Pull up a chair," Todd said, and Zack obliged. Then he looked around in distaste.

"Why are you meeting here?" he asked.

"Well, we can't meet at school," Todd said. "We were supposed to start meeting at Denny's, but something came up."

"My old man's home with the flu," Denny muttered.

"This place is pretty out of the way," Zack commented.

"I know," Todd said. "That's why the guys who don't have cars aren't here." He frowned. "It would be a lot easier if we could just meet at school. But there's no way Quimby's going to let us become an official school activity. The Pro-White Union is not exactly politically correct."

"I could work on that," Zack said. "I've been giving it some thought. There's no reason why being exclusive should keep the club from being recognized. Like I said before, the African American Students League is recognized, and that's exclusive. Over at the Middle School, the Boy Scouts and Girl Scouts have meetings. They're exclusive, too."

"What do we have to do to get recognized?" Kurt asked suspiciously. "I'm not about to start sucking up to those bleeding heart liberal administrators. What do you want to do, become respectable?"

"If it helps accomplish our goals," Todd replied. "I saw something on TV the other night, about this skinhead group in Germany. One of them let his hair grow, he put on a suit, and now he's running for a real government office!"

"If you want, I could write up a formal proposal for you," Zack offered. "I'll use lots of legal language. They like that kind of stuff."

"You know how to do that?" Denny asked.

"Sure, I can get one of my father's lawyers to help me out," Zack replied.

Todd eyed him thoughtfully. "Your father's a state senator, right?"

"Yeah, and he has a lot of clout. He's dead

set against affirmative action, you know. In fact, he's working on getting some of those laws changed."

It seemed to Zack that whenever he brought up his father's name in a class or at *Video High* meetings, people looked away and acted bored. Not these guys. All of them looked distinctly impressed.

The skinhead Zack didn't know spoke up. "It would be good to have a connection in high places."

"You're right, Frank," Todd said approvingly. "Zack, you really think you can get us officially recognized?"

Zack preened. "Sure. I can pull a few strings, and get my father to put some pressure on the school. And once the organization gets recognized, it can apply for funding from the student government."

"We sure could use that," Denny commented. "Spray paint ain't cheap."

"What do you need spray paint for?" Zack asked.

Denny leered. "Advertising. We're going to hit the side of the school building tonight. Want to help out?"

Zack couldn't quite picture himself painting graffiti on the school at midnight. "Uh, sorry, I'm busy. Look, if you're serious about getting recognized, I'm going to need some information." He opened a notebook. "First of all, you need to have a mission statement."

"What's that?" Todd asked.

"A general statement that says what you're all about."

"To push the minorities back in their place," Kurt said promptly.

"To keep the races separate," Frank offered.

"That sounds too hostile," Zack said. "Let me think . . . how about something like . . . the Pro-White Union was established to give white students an opportunity to reaffirm their racial identity and promote their culture."

"Cool," Denny said. "Sounds really professional."

"We'll need to list goals and objectives, too," Zack told them. Then he snapped his fingers. "I know. I'll get my hands on the proposal that established the African American Students League. I'll just change certain words. That way, if they try to turn us down, I can point out that the proposals are practically identical." He chuckled. "We could bring a discrimination suit against them!"

"Brilliant!" Todd exclaimed.

"But how are you going to get your hands on their proposal?" Brett asked.

"Easy," Zack replied. "Their proposal or constitution or whatever they call it has to be on file in the assistant principal's office. The secretary there knows me."

Brett was beaming at him. "I have a feeling you're going to be a real asset to this organization."

"I think he should be more than that," Todd said suddenly. "Let's make Zack president."

"Hold on," Kurt objected. "I thought we weren't going to have officers."

"We need a spokesperson," Todd stated. "Someone who looks right, talks right . . ."

"What's the matter with the way we look?" Kurt asked belligerently.

"Nothing," Todd said quickly. "But it scares some people."

Kurt stared at him defiantly. "So what? Some people need to be scared. And you know who I mean."

"I think we should make Zack president," Denny said.

"Me, too," Frank echoed. "Sorry, Kurt, but Todd's right."

"I agree," Brett piped up eagerly.

Zack was floored. This was much too easy. "Shouldn't you wait till all the members can meet and have a real election?" he asked tentatively.

Denny chortled. "What do you think this is, a democracy?"

Todd turned to Zack. "Okay, Mr. President, what do we do now?"

Zack was trying to recover from the shock of suddenly finding himself a proclaimed leader. He thought rapidly. "Well, first off, you want to start recruiting more members. Power comes from numbers. The more members you can get, the more influence you—we—can have."

Todd nodded. "I think there are a lot of kids out there who feel like we do."

"Yeah, they're just too wimpy to speak up for themselves," Denny commented.

"What have you done so far to get members?" Zack asked.

"Not much," Todd admitted. "Just flyers and posters. They haven't been very successful."

"But we've been making ourselves known in other ways," Kurt declared. He smiled wickedly. "We've scared a few folks with some notes. You know about Steve Nowicki and that colored girl?"

"Debra Lewis," Zack said. "Yeah. Pretty disgusting." He was about to tell them about Kris Hogan's interest in Howard Weller, but Kurt kept talking.

"Well, we've been letting them know we're watching them. And if they keep hanging out together, we're going to make some real threats."

Alarmed, Zack asked, "What kind of threats?"

"Oh, the usual stuff," Kurt said vaguely. "You know what I mean."

Zack didn't. But now he was glad he hadn't mentioned Kris. Much as she'd disgusted him, he didn't want her threatened.

"And we've got plans for more action,"

Denny added. "Like, maybe, burning some crosses on certain lawns. Like the Ku Klux Klan."

"And painting swastikas," Frank said. "Nazi symbols." He drew a figure in the air.

Zack couldn't believe what he was hearing. This sounded like the kind of stuff hoodlums and rednecks did. He glanced at Todd. Even that respectable-looking boy was nodding and smiling. So was Brett.

Zack's face must have revealed his reaction. Denny looked at him sharply. "What's the matter?"

"Nothing," Zack said hastily.

Denny defended himself anyway. "Look, we have to get attention, let people know we're around."

"Of course, this is small time stuff," Todd said. "We need to start thinking bigger, we have to reach more people."

Frank eyed Zack keenly. "You do that *Video High* show, don't you?"

"Yes."

"Television," Frank said. "That's what we need. If we could present our ideas on TV, think of the audience we'd reach! We could recruit more people with a few minutes on TV than we could with a million flyers."

"Brilliant!" Todd said. He turned to Zack. "Get us on *Video High*."

Zack averted his eyes. "But it's just a dumb

little cable show. I don't think so many people watch it."

"It's better than nothing," Denny stated. "It's not like we're going to get on *Sixty Minutes*. Not yet, at least."

"Yeah, *Video High* will do for a start," Kurt said.

Zack formulated his words carefully. "It's not that easy, you know. We plan the shows way in advance. I don't know when you can get on . . ." He was stalling for time, to think.

But they weren't going to give him any. "We don't need the whole show," Todd said. "You can get us five minutes, can't you? That's long enough to get our message across."

"Well, I'll see," Zack murmured. "I don't make the decisions. There's a whole group involved. And an advisor."

Kurt's eyes narrowed. "I thought you had influence in high places."

"Yeah, you're supposed to be such a big shot," Denny added. His voice carried an ominous undertone.

There was no way Zack was going to admit that he had very little influence on *Video High*. He swallowed, hard. "I'll see what I can do."

A burly man in a dirty white apron approached them. "You folks going to order anything?"

No one responded.

"You're taking up seats," the man barked. "Beat it."

That broke up the meeting. The boys ambled out of the diner.

"We'll meet Wednesday night, at Denny's," Todd told Zack. Everyone began heading to their cars.

"Can you give me a lift?" Brett asked Zack.

"Yeah."

Inside the car, Brett said, "You didn't sound too thrilled about the *Video High* idea."

"I don't know about these guys," Zack confessed as he pulled out of the parking space. "Making threats, burning crosses, painting swastikas . . ." He shuddered.

"I thought you liked what they stand for," Brett said.

"Sure, I'm all for supporting white guys, and letting people know how we've been victimized by the minorities. But that other stuff . . . it's pretty extreme."

He wasn't sure that he should be admitting all this to Brett. Despite the fact that they shared some opinions, he still thought Brett was a little nobody, a jerk who'd jump on any bandwagon that would have him.

But Brett didn't appear to be shocked by Zack's concerns. "You're the president now," he said. "You're the leader of this group. You can use your position to persuade them to cut out the pranks and concentrate on more meaningful stuff."

"You think so?" Zack asked doubtfully. "Guys like Denny and Kurt, I think they're really into the redneck scene. They're serious thugs."

"You can make them change," Brett said firmly. "You're a politician, and that's what politicians do, right? Convince people to do what you want them to do, think the way you want them to think."

"Yeah." And silently, he added, exactly what my father told me I had no talent for.

"Of course," Brett continued, "for now, you'll have to go along with them, to win their trust. You gotta act more enthusiastic. Once you get more members, the group is going to become really powerful. And you'll be a hero."

It was amazing to Zack, how he was actually taking advice from this dweeb. But he wanted to believe every word he was saying.

"You're getting a lot of respect from these guys, Zack." Brett paused. "But you'd better get them on *Video High*. At least, try real hard. Or you'll lose it."

Eight

Despite the fact that she was studying her *Romeo and Juliet* notes, Debra sensed her parents' eyes on her at the breakfast table Tuesday morning. She looked up and saw two worried faces.

"Honey, you haven't even touched your breakfast," her mother noted.

Debra glanced with disinterest at the bowl of cereal. "I'm not hungry, Mom."

"Is something bothering you?" her father asked.

Debra knew she had to come up with some explanation for her behavior. "I guess I'm just a little nervous about this presentation I'm giving today."

Mrs. Lewis seemed to accept that. "Is that the English assignment you've been working on with that boy we met—what's his name?"

"Steve Nowicki."

"Nice fellow," her father remarked.

"Yes, he is," Debra said. Impulsively, she asked, "Does it bother you that he's white?"

"Why would that bother us?" her mother asked. "You've always had white friends."

Then Debra noticed her father's eyebrows come together, a clear sign of concern. "Unless . . . are you going to tell us the young man is more than a friend?"

Debra hesitated. She didn't know if the worry in her father's eyes came from the idea of her having any sort of boyfriend, or a *white* boyfriend. In a voice that she hoped carried more assurance than she felt, she said, "No, it's nothing like that. He's just a friend."

She wasn't sure if her mother bought that. She could see a keen interest in her face, and she didn't think she could handle any more questions. It was so hard to keep things from them. She pushed back her chair. "I have to run. Steve and I are going to meet before homeroom."

The concerned faces of her parents lingered in her mind long after she left the house. She'd always been closer to her parents than most of her friends were. Maybe it had something to do with being an only child, and getting all their attention. She shared practically everything with them, her experiences and her feelings. She never lied to them.

But she hadn't been sharing much with them lately. When she told them she was nervous about performing her assignment, that wasn't exactly true.

It was ironic, in a way. When Mr. Russell

first announced the assignment, she had been totally unnerved at the prospect. Now, it was the least of her worries. Amazing, the changes one week could create.

There was so much her parents didn't know about her life now. They didn't know about the racist notes. They didn't know she was going to be on *Video High* this Thursday.

She was still stunned at the idea that she was going to do that. *Why* had she let Steve talk her into it? He'd been so persuasive. Her thoughts went back to the day before, and her mind conjured up a clear memory of his earnest expression, and his words.

"I can't bear the thought of those scumbags thinking they've scared us. We have to show them that they have no impact on what we do with our lives."

She didn't want to tell him about her shyness. But she didn't need to. She had another, more serious objection. "But if we go on TV and talk about it, it implies that we're taking them seriously."

They'd gone on like this for a while. Steve had been impassioned, he'd seemed to believe this was terribly important. And the more he spoke, so fervently, the more she felt her own resolutions waver. In a last-ditch effort not to give in, she'd brought up one more argument.

"I'm not sure that it's ethical for us to appear on TV as a couple, as if we're romantically involved. It would be . . . deceitful."

She would never forget his response to that: "It doesn't have to be."

So this was something else her parents weren't aware of—her confused feelings about Steve. Her bewildering, perplexing, and slightly exhilarating feelings.

But she refused to think about that now. Instead, she concentrated on how happy Sharon had been last night, when she'd learned Debra and Steve would be on the show. She had promised Debra she wouldn't ask her anything too intimate on the air, and that she wouldn't expect either of them to discuss their personal relationship.

"I'll just ask you about what the notes said, and your response to them," she had told Debra. And Debra felt reasonably certain that she would keep to her word. Sharon might do just about anything to make her show dramatic and exciting, but she wouldn't betray her best friend.

At school, she found Steve waiting for her in the library. The first words out of his mouth were, "I hope you're not angry at me."

"Why would I be angry?" Debra asked.

"For pressuring you into going on *Video High*. I know I came on too strong. I kept thinking about it last night. I even tried to call you, around ten, to let you know we could just forget about it. But your line was busy."

"I was talking to Sharon."

"Anyway," Steve went on, "if you want to

call it off, that's okay with me. I mean that, Debra."

He really did, she could see that. Everything about Steve was sincere and honest.

She was torn. Once again, she remembered how fervently he'd pleaded with her the day before. It was so very clear how much this meant to him. Then she thought about how disappointed Sharon would be if they dropped out.

And way, way back, in a tiny corner of her mind, there was the smallest flicker of an image, of a boy and a girl, together, in love, facing the forces that tried to tear them apart. Like Romeo and Juliet.

"It's okay," she said. "I don't mind, really. Now, let's get to work."

They only had twenty minutes to practice before the bell. But their work paid off. In English class, most of the other students stumbled over their lines, or broke into giggles in the middle of their presentations.

But their presentation went well. Debra had to consult her notes, and she knew her performance wasn't exactly theatrical, but she spoke clearly and distinctly. And as they got toward the end of their scene, her relief that it was almost over made the last part easy.

They were at the point where Romeo and Juliet had said goodbye, but then Juliet called him to come back.

"It will seem like twenty years until I see

you tomorrow," Debra read. "But now I've forgotten why I asked you to come back here."

"I'll stay here until you remember," Steve said.

"But then I'll forget again, because you're standing right there, and all I can think about is how much I love having you here."

"Then I'll stay while you forget again, and I've forgotten that I have any other home but this one."

"But it's almost morning," Debra said. "And you should leave. But I wish you wouldn't go very far, no farther than a captured bird, who hops out of a person's hand but comes right back."

"I will be your captured bird," Steve recited.

"And I'll be yours," Debra replied. "I just hope I don't kill you from holding you so tight! Good night, good night. Leaving you makes me feel so sad, but the sooner I say good night, the sooner it will be morning."

Her part was done, and she was able to watch Steve. And as Steve said his final words, she thought to herself, he's really getting into this. His tone carried the same intensity it had held the day before, when he'd said that appearing as a romantic couple might just not be a lie.

When Steve finished, the class broke into applause. They hadn't done that for any of the other presentations. Debra was pleased, but a little embarrassed, too. It wasn't so much from the applause, but the way some of her classmates were looking at them, with avid curiosity and knowing expressions.

"Excellent job," Mr. Russell proclaimed. "That was almost like watching a professional play."

He's exaggerating, Debra thought, at least, when it applied to *her*. But Steve had been terrific, like a real actor.

Or maybe, he wasn't acting.

And once again, she was deliciously confused.

"Come on, Debra," Sharon urged. "We'll be late for the meeting."

Debra took some books from her locker and slammed it shut. "I'm not going."

"To the *Video High* meeting? Why not?"

"Because I have to see my chemistry teacher about a project, and then I need to go to the library," Debra replied.

"But I'm bringing something up and I need your support," Sharon moaned.

Debra smiled and shook her head. "I'm sure you'll do just fine without me. You *always* get your way."

Sharon laughed. "But it's not always easy."

"Anyway," Debra went on, "I don't really need to be at the meeting today. I'm a guest this week, remember?"

"*I* remember," Sharon said. "I just hope *you* do."

Debra sighed. "How could I forget?"

Tyler joined them, and glanced at Debra's locker door. "You didn't get any of those notes today?"

"No, thank goodness," Debra said.

Sharon actually seemed a little disappointed. "That's too bad."

Appalled, Debra asked, "Why?"

"The more notes you can talk about on the show, the more dramatic it will be." Sharon met Debra's eyes, and saw that she'd have to defend her comment. "I'm just being practical! We want this show to have an impact, don't we?"

"Not if I have to suffer reading more of those notes for it," Debra shot back.

Sharon actually felt a little shame. "I'm sorry, Deb. Look, I know I sound like a raving lunatic. But racism is so evil. I want the world to wake up and recognize that. I want to make some changes!"

"Geez," Tyler said, "I have a feeling I'm going with Joan of Arc." He turned to Debra. "Am I ever going to get used to her and her causes?"

Debra laughed. "Tyler, she's been my best friend for ten years, and *I'm* not used to her."

Sharon responded good-naturedly. "Quit teasing me, you two. Deb, Tyler and I are going to the movies Friday night. You and Steve want to come with us?"

"I don't know," Debra said.

"Are you meeting him at the library?" Sharon asked.

"No, we're finished with the English assignment. I'm working on something for American History. There's no reason for me to meet Steve there."

"I just thought you might like to be with him," Sharon said. "Is that so bizarre?"

"Good grief, Sharon, we're not exactly joined at the hip," Debra retorted.

"Well, I still wish you were coming to the meeting, and bringing Steve, too," Sharon commented. "I could have used the support."

"Support for what?" Tyler asked.

There was a sparkle in Sharon's eyes as she said, "I've got a fabulous idea for Thursday. Something to make the show just a little more interesting."

"Uh-oh," Tyler said. "What is it this time, an armed uprising?"

Sharon grinned. "I'm not going to tell you. It'll be a surprise."

They were nearing the studio. "I'll see you," Debra said, but she paused as Jade joined them. Jade congratulated Debra on her English presentation. "I heard it was terrific."

"Who'd you hear that from?" Debra asked.

"Some kids in one of my classes who were in your class. They said it was *very* convincing.

They thought they were watching a real Romeo and Juliet." She gave Debra a leer.

Debra didn't rise to the bait. "Steve's a good actor," she replied simply. "See ya."

Sharon went into the studio and began looking around the room, checking out who was there and who she could count on for support today. Coming up the risers was someone she knew she wouldn't get any support from at all. After all, he'd been opposed to the topic in the first place. But she was in such a good mood, she managed a brief smile and greeted him anyway.

"Hi, Zack."

She expected one of his usual sneers, and maybe a snotty comment on the topic of her upcoming show. Instead, he gazed at her vaguely, as if his mind was a million miles away.

"Hi, Sharon," he murmured, and moved on up the risers.

Jade had observed this brief encounter. "He looks weird. I mean, weirder than usual. Like he's sick or something."

"Mm," Sharon agreed. She was too preoccupied with her own concerns to give Zack much thought.

Tyler, though, had twisted his head to watch Zack, and he shook his head. "That is one strange guy. I'll never figure him out."

Sharon turned to him. "Why? Just because he said hello to me?"

"It's not that. You know who I saw him talking to this morning? Denny Banks and some other skinhead."

That bit of information caught Sharon's interest. "Oh yeah? Did you hear what they were talking about?"

"No. I was just surprised to see them together."

Jade had been listening to this exchange. "Why? You know how right wing he is."

Tyler considered that. "He's conservative, sure, but I never would put him in the same category as those thugs. He's not exactly a racist; he's too straight. I don't think he likes any kind of extremism."

Sharon thought Tyler's surprise was exaggerated. "Just because he was talking to them doesn't mean he's hanging out with them."

"It was still pretty strange," Tyler insisted. "You know how conscious he is of his position and his image and who he's seen with. Something weird is going on."

Sharon dismissed that. "You're making a mountain out of a molehill."

"Look who's talking," Tyler retorted.

Sharon wasn't about to dignify that with an answer, only a withering look. *She* didn't do that, make mountains out of molehills. Why didn't anyone understand that she simply wanted to change the world? That she wanted to make this a better place for people. And she'd do anything to achieve those goals.

In her opinion, they should all be grateful for her commitment. After all, if it hadn't been for her, they wouldn't even be able to do this show on Thursday.

Debra had a brief meeting with her teacher, and then went down the stairs to the library. As she neared the door, coming out were two girls, seniors, she knew vaguely. She smiled a greeting.

They paused, exchanged looks with each other, and the taller girl spoke. "You're Debra Lewis, aren't you?"

"Yes." She wracked her brain for the girl's name. "You're Laney, right?"

"Yes, I talked to you once about the African American Students League. I'm the vice-president." She indicated her friend. "This is Donna."

Donna wasn't smiling. "You're the one who's going with the white guy, right?"

Debra was taken aback. "Well, we've been out together. I wouldn't say we're actually going together."

"That's not what I heard," Donna retorted. "I hear you two are going hot and heavy."

Debra was distinctly annoyed by her words, but she tried to sound calm. "Excuse me, but I don't know if that's any of your business."

Laney spoke more gently. "Maybe not,

Debra. But as black women, we have to be concerned."

"Why?"

"Do you know how this looks?" Laney asked.

Donna, scowling, added, "It's a slap in the face to black men."

Debra gazed at her in bewilderment. "What are you talking about? That's ridiculous!"

"What's the matter, aren't black guys good enough for you?" Donna challenged her.

Debra drew herself up stiffly. "Just because I went out with Steve doesn't mean I wouldn't go out with a black guy."

"Then why don't you?" Donna asked.

"None of them ever asked me!" Debra replied.

"That's irrelevant," Donna sniffed.

"Listen, Debra," Laney said, "you have to consider what people are going to think when they see you with a white guy. It's—it's like you're betraying your own people. Like you take no pride in being an African American." Her deep brown eyes were soft and pleading.

But Donna's eyes were flashing. "Are you going to go on seeing him?"

"Why shouldn't I?" Debra replied hotly. "He's my friend. I care about him."

Laney sighed. "Well, if that's how you feel. . . . We just wanted to share our feelings with you. People *are* talking, you know.

I wish you'd just think about it, okay?" They started away, but Donna looked back.

"You're a disgrace to all black people," she snapped.

Debra remained where she was, in a state of shock, watching them until they turned a corner and disappeared from view. Even then, she couldn't move.

She felt sick, upset, and unable to think clearly. A couple of students passed, and glanced at her curiously. That's when she became aware that tears were falling down her face.

She'd forgotten what she needed from the library. She forced herself to move, without even knowing where she was going. Eventually, she found herself near the gym, where a bank of pay telephones stood.

She fumbled in her purse for a coin. As she was about to insert it, she realized she had no idea who she was about to call. And then, she did.

"Hello, Steve? It's Debra."

He must have heard the trembling in her voice, because immediately he asked, "What's wrong?"

"I . . . um, something happened. These people, they said something . . ."

"The skinheads?" he asked sharply.

"No . . ." She couldn't keep the tears back, and she couldn't keep a sob from escaping her lips.

"Where are you?" Steve asked.

"At school."

"I'll pick you up by the gym door."

Sharon was getting impatient. It seemed to her that they were spending a lot of time, too much time, discussing the possible topics for future shows.

But at last, attention was directed to Thursday's program. "Kris, do you have a report for us?" Jeff asked.

Kris, who was sitting just behind Sharon, got up. "As you know, I'm going to be interviewing Howard Weller, and we'll be discussing his Outstanding Senior award. I'll ask him about what he's done to deserve it, his school activities and community work, what his future plans are, and all that."

"Are you going to discuss what he's accomplished as student body president?" Jeff asked.

"I asked Howard about that," Kris said. "And he said he thought we should hold off on that until we can have all the student body officers on the show. He said he doesn't want to be taking all the credit for what student government does."

"That's a good point," Jeff remarked. "Maybe we should devote a segment of a future show to student government."

Sharon twisted around in her seat to look at Kris. Kris's eyes were hazy and dreamy.

"Howard is so humble," Kris declared in rapture. "He's not the least bit conceited at all."

"Are you going to need an entire half hour for the interview?" Sharon asked.

"No," Kris told her. "Just fifteen minutes, I think. Howard says that since he's going to be part of your panel, too, he would prefer to share more of the time with the others. He thinks a panel is going to be more interesting to the audience than him alone." She sighed deeply. "He's so unselfish, he's always thinking of other people."

Sharon nudged Jade, and whispered, "She met him once and now she's madly in love. Can you believe it?"

"I have a pretty good feeling it's all in her head," Jade said. "I think Debra and Steve are still the only official interracial couple at Greenwood."

"Sharon, can you give us a report?" Jeff asked.

Sharon rose. "For the panel on race relations, I've got David Philby, who's the president of the African American Students League, Dr. Danielle Parsons from the school board, and Howard Weller. I'm going to ask them about the state of race relations among young people, why there's been some conflict and how we can prevent that. And we'll talk about how race relations can be improved in city schools."

"Good," Jeff said.

"And, I plan to have an interracial couple

who are going to talk about the pressures they've experienced from the Pro-White Union."

Jeff frowned. "The what?"

Some other students seemed puzzled, too. It dawned on Sharon that not everyone had seen the posters or the flyers. "It's a group of students who . . ." She wasn't exactly sure how to describe these people. "I guess you could call them white supremacists. They've been putting out flyers about white pride and how minorities are taking over and all that. They've sent some nasty notes to this couple I mentioned."

"Are you serious?" Jeff asked. "This couple has actually received threats?"

"The notes don't actually threaten them," Sharon admitted. "But they're very racist."

Jeff made an expression of distaste. "All right, that should be interesting." Then he glanced at the notes he'd been taking. "Do you think you've got enough here to fill the period? Remember, you've got forty-five minutes for your segment now. Do you need more panelists?"

This was the opening Sharon had been waiting for. "I've been thinking about that, and I've got an idea. I think this could make the show a lot more stimulating. Thought provoking." She paused, took a deep breath, and said, "I'd like to invite members of the Pro-White Union to be on the panel."

A murmur went through the group. Several kids turned to face Sharon, and most of them looked aghast.

"The Pro-White Union?" Jeff stared at Sharon with undisguised astonishment. "You mean, that supremacist group you were just talking about?"

"Yes. I thought they could talk about why they formed their group, what their philosophy is, what they want to accomplish, that sort of thing. The other panelists could respond to them. It would be like a debate! Don't you think that would be a lot more exciting?"

"Maybe too exciting," said a voice close to her.

Sharon looked at Jade. "What do you mean?"

Jade got up. "All I'm saying is that when you put people like that on TV, things can get out of control. Did you hear about what happened on that talk show a couple of years ago? There were black people and members of the Ku Klux Klan on it, and they had buddies in the audience. Someone in the audience got furious, and they all went wild."

"I remember that show," someone else said. "They were yelling and screaming and carrying on, and someone in the audience threw a chair at the host! I think his nose was broken."

"We don't have chairs," Sharon replied. "I don't think anyone in the audience is going to try and throw bleachers."

Jeff was impassive. "Let's hear more thoughts on this," he said.

Spencer Kelly, in the front row, got up. "I agree with Jade. A show like this could get very dangerous. We could all be at risk."

Sharon groaned. She figured Spencer was only saying that because she'd gone out with him once and it hadn't gone too well. But she couldn't tell that to the group. Instead, she simply dismissed his objection.

"They're not going to be armed," she said. "Besides, they're all talk. I don't think they've done anything violent."

"You don't know that," a guy remarked. "And there's always a first time."

"They're Greenwood students," Sharon protested. "They have a right to be heard."

"Sharon, why are you standing up for racists?" someone asked.

"I'm not standing up for them," Sharon replied indignantly. "Personally, I think they're disgusting. But we're supposed to present all points of view on this show." She directed herself to Jeff. "Isn't that right?"

Jeff spoke slowly and deliberately. "To some extent, yes. But if I understand correctly what this group is all about, then what they're promoting is contrary to our civil rights laws. I'm not sure that we're obliged to give them air time."

Sharon had an answer for that. "Because what they're promoting is against the law?

Just a few weeks ago, when we had that show about drug pushers, we had someone sitting right on that stage who advocated legalizing marijuana. *That's* against the law, too!"

Kris Hogan was frantically flapping her hand in the air. "This could ruin my interview," she wailed. "Howard Weller isn't going to want to be on the same stage as racists!"

"How do you know?" Sharon fired back. "He might appreciate the opportunity to confront his enemies. That's important for all of us! We need to know more about these people so we can stop them."

"I think we know enough about them already," one of the students said.

"But there might be people watching on TV who don't!" Sharon declared. "They may have no idea that such dangerous groups exist in high schools. Come on, everyone, we've never been afraid of controversy before."

Another student rose, and she looked positively furious. "We get one hour a week to inform people in this city about our concerns. There's no way we should give one minute of that time to scumbag skinheads!"

"I don't even want people to know we've got students like that at Greenwood!" another kid yelled.

"That's the same argument people used when we wanted Jade to be on the show!" Sharon yelled back. She looked to Jade for some support. But Jade shook her head.

"That's entirely different," Jade declared firmly. "What I'm all about doesn't hurt people. *They* do!"

A scattering of applause went through the room, which only made Sharon more angry. "We have to face facts! Even if we don't approve of them, we have to admit they exist!"

"Hey, hold it, folks, let's stay calm," Jeff called out loudly. "There's no need for shouting. Is there anyone here who supports Sharon's idea?"

Sharon gazed around the suddenly silent studio. To her amazement, Zack stood up.

Usually, when Zack had something to say at these meetings, his voice boomed and he went on talking at some length. But not this time.

"I don't think it's such a bad idea," he mumbled. "There's such a thing as freedom of speech." Then, abruptly, he sat back down.

It wasn't much, Sharon thought, but it was something. Never, in a million years, could she have anticipated Zack's words. She couldn't remember any other time when he'd taken her side in an issue.

She gave him her biggest smile. But he was hunched over, staring at the floor, and didn't see her.

"If they want freedom of speech, let them get their own show," a boy declared.

"Anyone else have a comment?" Jeff asked.

Tyler stood up. *Finally*, Sharon thought. Tyler didn't talk a lot at these meetings, but when he did speak, his comments were always thoughtful and people listened to him.

"I think," he said slowly, "that what Sharon's proposing to do is interesting, and provocative, and it would definitely make for a very dramatic program."

"Thank you," Sharon started to say, but Tyler wasn't finished.

"I have one concern, though. I keep thinking that if we give these people air time, it's like we're legitimizing them."

"Could you expand on that?" Jeff asked.

"This Pro-White Union—it isn't exactly a significant force here at Greenwood. They don't have many members. I think this could set a bad precedent."

"How?" Sharon asked.

"Well, what if a few students here suddenly decided to advocate . . . oh, I don't know, let's say turning Greenwood into an all male school. Or instituting a required school religion. We don't have to give every crackpot in the school time to state their case on *Video High*, do we?"

He had a point, even Sharon grudgingly admitted that. And she felt like she'd run out of arguments.

"And besides," another girl said, "if we let them on the show, we'd be playing right into their hands, giving them exactly what they want. Attention."

A general buzz of agreement rose from the group. Jeff turned to Sharon with a sympathetic smile. "I'm sorry, Sharon, but it looks like the group's not too crazy about your idea. Okay, folks, we've still got some other business to attend to. I'd like to hear some preliminary reports on next week's show."

Sharon sank down in her seat, and tried not to look like she was sulking.

By the time Steve arrived at school, Debra had managed to pull herself together. She got into the car, and he drove it to the far end of the school parking lot.

He parked the car there, and turned to her. "What happened?" he asked.

She told him about the encounter with Laney and Donna. She thought she'd be able to talk about it calmly and rationally. But as she went on, and tried to describe her feelings, fresh tears poured forth.

"They acted like I'd committed some terrible crime," she wept. "They made me feel so ashamed."

"You've done nothing to be ashamed of," Steve declared. He put an arm around her, and she rested her head against his chest. Despite her distress, she was aware of the fact that she'd never been in a position like this before. It was such a comfort to be held.

"You've got a right to be with anyone you want to be with," Steve said.

"I know that," Debra said through her

tears. "But they kept talking about how it looked to other people when they saw me with you."

"To hell with other people," Steve fumed. "We don't need any of them."

"They said I have no black pride. They said I should stop seeing you."

"You won't, will you? You aren't going to stop seeing me, right?"

Even though she couldn't see his face, she could hear the alarm in his voice. "No . . ."

"You want to be with me, don't you, Debra?"

With her head on his chest, Debra could hear the pounding of his heart. "Yes."

"Because when I'm with you, I feel . . . oh, I don't know how to describe it. I feel like I can *talk* to you, in a way I've never been able to communicate with any other girl."

"It's the same for me," Debra said softly. That was the truth. She'd never been able to talk to a boy as easily as she talked to Steve.

"We won't let anyone stand in our way," he declared fiercely. "Will we?"

Debra's own heartbeat quickened. "Stand in the way of what?"

"Our love."

She took her head off his chest and looked up at him. "Oh, Steve. It's too soon . . ."

But he wasn't listening. "People talk about having pride in their race," he mused. "That's okay, I guess, but not if it tears people apart." He bent his head to meet her eyes. "We can take pride in *us*, Debra. The way we stay together, and tough it out, no matter what anyone says or does."

Debra's tears were gone, but now her head was spinning. "Steve," she began.

"Sh," he said soothingly. And then he kissed her.

Nine

Zack was on his way out of the *Video High* meeting when Sharon called to him. "Zack, wait."

He stopped, and she hurried over to him. "I wanted to thank you for supporting me," she said.

"It's okay," he said, looking past her. He'd always thought Sharon was too aggressive for a girl. He didn't mind arguing with her, but when she was being nice like this, she made him feel uneasy.

"There's something I want to ask you," she began, and that *really* made him nervous. He was afraid she was going to ask about his interest in the Pro-White Union, and he'd have to come up with a reasonable explanation. He wasn't about to acknowledge his participation until the group became more . . . what was the phrase Tyler had used? More of a significant force.

But fortunately, her friends were heading her way, and she was distracted. "You're not angry at us, are you?" Jade asked her. "I had to say what I thought. You understand, don't you?"

"Sure, I understand," Sharon said cheerily.

Zack was surprised. Sharon always struck him as so emotional, and she took her causes very seriously. He'd seen her anger when she didn't get her way.

She didn't give up easily. It was another thing about her that made him uncomfortable.

"You want to go to Harry's?" Tyler was asking her.

"In a minute, I need to talk to Zack first," she said.

"Look, I have to go," Zack said in a rush, and he ran out before she could stop him.

He had parked his car at the far end of the school parking lot, and it was there that he saw them—Debra Lewis and Steve Nowicki, huddled together in the front seat of a car, and they were kissing.

He averted his eyes. Disgusting, he thought. He jumped into his own car, gunned the motor, and tore out of the parking lot as fast as he could.

The races shouldn't mix like that, he fumed. It was wrong, it was unnatural. People should stick with their own kind. Of course, those liberals in *Video High* probably wouldn't be bothered by what he'd just seen. At least the Pro-White Union would understand how he felt.

But he wasn't sure if he should tell them. He remembered them talking about the notes they'd been sending Steve and Debra. They could escalate their attack, turn the notes into threats, and maybe take action on those threats.

What would the Pro-White Union do to them, he wondered. On the one hand, he certainly didn't like the idea of a racially mixed couple. But on the other hand, he didn't really want to see them get hurt. It wasn't hard to picture guys like Kurt and Denny and Frank ganging up on Steve. And what would they do to Debra? He didn't want to think about that.

He'd never felt so utterly confused in his life.

When he'd realized, at the *Video High* meeting, that the Pro-White Union wouldn't be invited to appear on the show, his first reaction had been one of immense relief. He was off the hook. He'd done what he could, by supporting Sharon's idea—not very enthusiastically, but at least he could honestly tell them he'd tried.

But in complete honesty, he had to admit to himself, he hadn't wanted the Pro-White Union to go on *Video High*. He didn't want to hear any more about burning crosses and making threats and painting swastikas.

He tried to concentrate on what Brett advised him to do—to go along with them, be a strong leader, and turn them around, point them in a more respectable direction. They could take more positive actions to improve the status of white people. Like—like—what? He couldn't think of anything.

Maybe his father could give him advice, some ideas. But then his stomach began churning as he contemplated approaching the senator. Ever since last Tuesday, when his father lectured him on what a failure he was, they'd had little contact. Conversations were limited to the dinner table, and essentially consisted of "pass the salt, please."

But here was an opportunity to show his father that he *was* taking steps to become a leader. The senator probably wouldn't be too impressed by the fact that he was now president of a ragtag bunch of skinheads and assorted racists. But Zack could exaggerate the size of the group, and downplay the sleaziness of some of its members.

He could point out that he was getting in on the ground floor of this organization, and indicate his intention to expand it and build it into something grand. *That* should get his father to take Zack seriously.

There was no one at home when he got there. He had just entered his bedroom when his phone rang.

"Hello?"

"Hey, Stevenson, this is Todd. I just wanted to remind you about the meeting tonight at

Denny's. We sent around some flyers today but they got confiscated by some lousy teacher. You got the address?"

Zack jotted it down as Todd recited it. "What time?" he asked.

"Eight," Todd told him. "But be sure to check the driveway when you get there. If there's a blue station wagon parked in it, don't come in."

"Why not?"

"Denny's parents don't exactly approve of us. They're supposed to be out tonight, but just in case . . ."

"Okay, I got it."

"Did you have a *Video High* meeting today?" Todd asked.

"Yeah." He thought quickly. He hadn't yet completely decided how to handle what he knew would be the next question. He hit a button on the phone to make a clicking sound. "That's my call waiting. I'll give you the whole story tonight, okay?"

He hung up the phone. Just then, he heard the front door slam. He left his room and went down the hall.

"Hello, Father."

Senator Stevenson grunted something that barely came close to a greeting.

"Could I talk to you for a minute?" he asked.

His father made no effort to conceal his reluctance, but he nodded. Zack followed him into his study.

"What do you want?" the senator asked gruffly.

"I'm, uh, you see, there's this group, it's new, at school, and, and, I'm the president, they made me president . . ." He was stammering, he could hear himself. He had to pull himself together.

"It's called the Pro-White Union, and its mission is to give white students an opportunity to reaffirm their racial identity and promote their culture." He was enormously pleased that he was able to recall the phrase he'd composed for the group.

He tried to read the expression on the senator's face, but it was a total blank. Still, his father was listening, and that was something.

"I need to help them get on the right track," Zack went on. "I think this group can be a significant force."

"What kind of people are in it?" the senator asked.

"Different kinds," Zack said vaguely, but he knew that answer wouldn't satisfy his father. "Some are more, more extreme than the others. You know, skinheads. They're a little wild. They're not going to be easy to lead."

"Nothing worthwhile is ever easy," his father stated.

"Oh, I know that," Zack said hastily. "But some of the things they want to do, they're scary." He immediately knew scary was the wrong word. His father's eyes had narrowed. "I mean, uh, you know."

"No, I don't know," the senator snapped irritably. "Get to the point." He was losing patience, that was evident. Zack could feel himself coming undone.

"They—they want to burn crosses on lawns, and paint swastikas on the school, and threaten interracial couples, and—and I don't know how to control them, how to stop them from doing dumb stuff like that."

"You can't take charge?" his father asked grimly. "Is that the problem?"

"Well, sort of, I mean, I'm not exactly sure. I have to figure out how to do it, how to make them listen to me, what to say to them. And I, I have to come up with some new ideas, projects for them to do, but I can't think of anything, and—" He stopped. That awful look was coming over his father's face again. There was no other word for it but contempt.

"Don't you have any gumption at all?" he shouted. "Are you telling me you can't even take charge of a lousy bunch of pranksters?"

"They're not all pranksters," Zack broke in, but his father hadn't finished.

"You just can't cut it, can you?"

"I want to try," Zack said in despair.

"Forget it," the senator snapped. "You might as well give up now. Tell your pathetic gang you can't play anymore." He sat down at his desk, and began going through his briefcase.

"Why do you call them pathetic?" Zack asked, his voice trembling.

His father looked up and glared at him. "They made you president, didn't they?"

Zack turned and left the study. He went back to his bedroom, and collected his car keys.

For almost an hour, he drove aimlessly. He didn't want to think. He even turned on the radio full blast, in the hope that the noise might drum all thoughts from his head.

But it was hard to reject one thought, one very certain absolute fact, a revelation, which was the result of this conversation with his father.

He was never going to win his father's respect. Or his love. No matter what he did, no matter how hard he tried.

And why? Zack knew the answer. Because he didn't deserve it. Everything his father said about him was true. He had no gumption. He was a coward. He couldn't even lead a mangy bunch of ignorant rednecks.

How could he ever expect to tell them how to act, what to think? When he wasn't even capable of making those decisions for himself.

He felt drained. He stopped at a fast food place, and ate a hamburger. It did nothing to fill his emptiness. But at least it was something to do, a way to kill time until it was almost eight o'clock.

As he turned down Denny's street, he remembered he was supposed to be on the alert for a blue station wagon. He wasn't sure if he wanted to see it or not.

The station wagon wasn't there. He got out of his car and went to the door.

Kurt opened it. His grunted greeting was similar to Senator Stevenson's. He really was an awful-looking guy, Zack thought. His watery blue eyes didn't hold the slightest spark of intelligence. He wore a ripped leather vest, open, with nothing underneath. Why would anyone want to bare a scrawny, sunken chest like that, Zack wondered. Kurt smelled, too, like he hadn't bathed in days.

Frank was slouched on the living room sofa. He looked pretty ugly too. He was scratching a tattoo on his arm. "I just got this," he announced proudly. It was a skull and crossbones, but that was barely visible since it was red and scabby.

"We're meeting in Denny's room," Kurt said. Frank rose, and they were led downstairs. They passed through a rec room. Denny's bedroom was just off it.

About seven guys were sprawled on the twin beds and all over the floor of the tiny room. "Zack, hi," Brett called. A couple of others mumbled greetings.

"Does everyone know Zack Stevenson?"

Todd asked. "He's our new president." He proceeded to introduce some of the others, but Zack wasn't really listening. He was looking around the room, and what he saw was hard to absorb.

It shouldn't have surprised him so much. He knew what Denny was into. But it shocked him nonetheless.

There were two huge posters. One portrayed a Ku Klux Klan gathering, with people in white hoods and robes standing around a burning cross. The other poster was an enlarged photograph of Adolf Hitler, his hand raised in the Nazi salute. Between the posters was a Confederate flag. Above this was a banner which proclaimed "White Power." And on the facing wall, Denny had painted a huge black swastika.

Nausea rose within him. The smell of cigarettes didn't help. He resisted an enormous urge to throw up.

"Have a seat," Denny drawled. "If you can find a space."

"It's too crowded in here," Frank complained.

"It'll be better when we can start meeting at school," Todd said. "Zack, have you done any work on that proposal to get us recognized?"

"I've started on it," Zack lied. "It'll take a little time. I want to get it right." He perched himself on the edge of a desk. "Um, I guess

I'd better call this meeting to order. Is there any old business to discuss?"

A couple of guys hooted. "What's this, parliamentary procedure?" one of them said. "We don't want to mess with that crap."

"It helps to be organized," Zack said lamely.

Brett stood up for him. "Yeah, we should listen. This guy knows what he's doing."

Zack fought back an irresistible, insane desire to laugh at this compliment. It only served to confirm his opinion of Brett, what a fool he was.

"Any old business?" he repeated.

"Yeah, I got some old business," a boy said. Having not listened to Todd's introductions, Zack had no idea what his name was.

The boy went on. "What happened to the swastikas that were supposed to be painted on the school last night?"

"I ran out of paint," Kurt said. "But I got a great idea, I think—"

"That's new business," Zack interrupted. "We're not through with old business."

"Gimme a break," Kurt muttered.

"Any more old business?" Todd asked. There didn't appear to be any, so he moved on. "New business?"

"I got some more paint," Kurt said. "But listen to this idea. Instead of wasting the paint on the school, I want to use it on a cemetery."

"A cemetery?" Zack was nonplussed. "Why?"

"I'm going to paint the tombstones," Kurt said. "Anyone want to help?"

"Wait a minute, I don't get it," Denny said. "Why do you want to paint swastikas on tombstones?"

Kurt grinned. "It's a Jewish cemetery."

"Hey, cool," a guy said. "I'll bet that gets us on the TV news."

Zack was dizzy. "But that's, that's desecration."

"It's what?" Kurt asked.

"Never mind," Zack said tiredly.

The doorbell rang. "I'll get it," Denny said, and left.

"I also got some ideas for that Nowicki guy," Kurt said. "The one who's dating the black girl. I'll start off with some small business. I could let the air out of his tires, pour sugar in his gas tank . . ."

"That's kid stuff," Zack blurted out. "Dumb little pranks. What's the point?"

But before anyone could respond, Denny returned. Zack glanced up to see who was with him. Then his mouth fell open.

"Sharon! What are you doing here?"

"Zack!" She gasped. "You—you're a member of this group?" It was very clear that she was just as stunned to see him as he was to see her.

"He's president," Todd said. "Who the hell are you?"

"I'm Sharon Delaney." For once, Sharon actually seemed ill at ease. She stood there stiffly, and Zack thought she looked tense. He watched as her eyes swept the room. They widened as she took in the items on the walls.

When she spoke, her voice was strained. "I have something to ask you all."

"You're a friend of that colored girl," Frank blurted out. "I've seen you with her at school."

"What girl are you talking about?" Sharon asked coolly.

"The one who goes with Steve Nowicki."

"Debra Lewis," Sharon said. "Yes, she's a friend of mine." She must have recognized the hostility in their reaction to this, because she proceeded quickly. "That's got nothing to do with why I'm here."

Brett broke in. "How did you know we were meeting here?"

Sharon fumbled in her jeans pocket and pulled out a paper. "I found this flyer at school. Look, can I get to the point? You don't want me here, and I don't want to stay here any longer than I have to." She looked at Zack, and he could feel the chill from her eyes. "Do I have your permission?"

He was too frozen to speak. He just nodded.

"I want to invite members of your group to appear on *Video High* this Thursday," she said.

"Hey, *all right!*" Todd exclaimed.

"Not all of you, of course," Sharon said. "You can choose two representatives."

Zack stared at her in disbelief. "Sharon,"

he began, but she continued as if he hadn't spoken.

"You'll be on a panel with some other people."

"What other people?" someone asked.

Zack watched Sharon twist her hands. She was very obviously nervous. Observing this didn't give him as much pleasure as he thought it would.

"Howard Weller," she said. "David Philby, and some other people."

"We gonna get equal time?" Denny asked.

"Yes," Sharon replied. "Make sure the two members you pick are in the studio at three o'clock on Thursday." With that, she turned and walked out.

Zack hopped off the desk. "I'll be right back," he told the group, and hurried out. He caught up with Sharon at the front door.

"What's going on?" he asked. "I thought you weren't going to be able to do this."

Sharon wouldn't meet his eyes. "I think it's important for an audience to hear these goons," she said. "Too many people think there's no racial problem at Greenwood. I'm going to show them they're wrong."

"But Jeff said—"

"I'm going over Jeff's head," she stated. "It's for the good of the show. The students at Greenwood need to be aware of who their enemies are. Excuse me." She tried to get past him but he blocked her way.

He could barely get the words out. "Sharon, I have to ask you a favor."

"What?"

Oh, how he hated being in this position. "Don't tell anyone you saw me here. Please."

Sharon finally looked at him directly. "Why? Aren't you proud of your organization?" Her voice dripped with sarcasm. "You're the president, Zack."

Pleading wouldn't work with a girl like this, Zack knew that. Besides, he wasn't going to sink that low. He tried a different tactic. Blackmail.

"Do you want Jeff Russell to know you went over his head before the show goes on? He can stop it, you know."

Sharon opened her mouth to speak, then closed it.

"We can make a deal," Zack said. "You keep my secret, I'll keep yours."

She was silent for a moment. Then she said, "Okay." And she left the house.

Zack went back to Denny's bedroom.

"Good work, Stevenson!" Todd said. "Why didn't you tell us you got us on the show?"

Zack tried to smile, but the muscles didn't seem to work. "Well, it's Sharon's segment, so she's the one who does the official invitation."

"This is totally cool," another boy said, and the others echoed this. Brett got up and slapped him on the back. Congratulations flew at him.

Throughout all this, Zack couldn't say anything. He accepted the praise silently. And all the time, he fought back the waves of nausea that threatened to engulf him.

Ten

On Thursday morning, Debra's alarm clock began ringing at the same time it always did—seven A.M. Automatically, she flung out an arm and shut it off. Normally, at this point, she would leap out of bed and head to the bathroom. But today, like the day before, she just lay there and stared up at the ceiling.

Had she dreamed about Steve that night, she wondered. She couldn't remember. But now, with her eyes wide open, his face was firmly implanted in her head. Not just his face—hers, too. His face and her face, together, kissing.

In the past, every now and then, she'd allowed herself to daydream about having a boyfriend. In her daydreams, the boy had been faceless, formless, nameless. It wasn't all that hard to replace the invisible fantasy with Steve.

So now she had a real live boyfriend, for the first time in her life. With effort, she could recall the sensations of his lips on hers, his arms around her. It had been nice—cozy and comforting, and she'd felt completely safe and secure.

Was that how it was supposed to feel? She'd always imagined there would be something else—bells, electricity, a shiver up and down her spine. Cozy and comforting weren't the words she'd ever heard to describe love. Wasn't love supposed to be associated with words like passion, rapture, ecstasy?

But maybe that was all just fantasy, notions that sprang from movies and love songs. Steve was the real thing. At least, that's what everyone else seemed to think. At least three times the day before, kids at school had stopped her to make some sort of remark about her and Steve being a couple. They'd gone out of their way to make it clear that they approved of the relationship. Debra supposed she should be happy about that, knowing there were plenty of students who weren't bothered by the idea of an interracial couple.

Then why had she been so uncomfortable, every time anyone spoke to her about it? The kind words had bothered her almost as much as the nasty notes from the Pro-White Union.

Steve . . . he wasn't bothered by kind words at all. He was such a nice guy. He'd called her last night, and she could still hear his words.

"It's going to be okay, Debra. Better than okay. We're going to be a symbol for people. We're going to show the world that love conquers all obstacles." Such sweet words, so romantic—but where were the shivers and the bells?

"My boyfriend, Steve," she said aloud, experimentally, rolling the words around her mouth. It sounded so strange. Maybe it was all just too new, too unfamiliar. Maybe it would just take a while for her to get used to the idea.

"Debra! Breakfast!"

"Coming, Mom."

She dressed quickly, with only a fleeting regard to the fact that she'd be on television that day. At least thinking about Steve for the past few days had completely occupied her mind, leaving little time to worry about her appearance on *Video High*. But as she went down the hall to the kitchen, she began to think about that.

She still hadn't mentioned anything about it to her parents. She didn't need to worry about them seeing the show—they'd both be at work. But then a thought struck her. What if someone they knew saw the program and told them about it? Debra was about to appear on TV as one half of an interracial couple. If her parents heard about this from someone else, they'd be shocked. She decided she'd better prepare them.

Her mother was at the stove, scrambling eggs in a pan.

"I hope those aren't for me," Debra said. "I'm not very hungry."

"They *are* for you, and you *will* eat them," her mother replied. "You haven't been eating well at all lately, and I've been worried about you."

"I'm fine," Debra said listlessly, but she didn't object when her mother placed the eggs before her. This was no time for an argument. "Where's Dad?"

"He's already left for work. We finally hired someone, and he's gone to the laundry to train him."

Debra was relieved. It would be easier to talk to her mother alone. But she had to approach this topic very, very carefully, and not leap into it. She had to sound casual. Maybe she could begin by talking generally about love, relationships . . .

"Mom . . ."

"Yes?"

"How did you feel when you first started dating Dad?"

Her mother's back was to her as she cleaned the kitchen counter. But Debra could tell she was considering her response. "Oh, I was happy. More than happy, exhilarated. I felt dizzy, like I was floating above the ground." She turned around and faced Debra. "Is that how you feel about Steve?"

Debra gasped. "Mom!" She began fumbling with her words. "Why do you—whatever makes you think—"

"You're my daughter and I know you," Mrs. Lewis said simply. "You've been walking around in a fog, you haven't been eating, you're not saying much to your father and me—what else could I think?"

Debra was about to protest, but what was the point? All she could offer her mother was a wan smile. Mrs. Lewis sat down at the table.

"Is it serious, Debra?"

"I don't know. I like him. He likes me. And—" But before she could get any farther, the phone rang. Her mother snatched it up.

"Hello?" After a pause, she said, "It's in the third cabinet, dear. No, on the bottom shelf. Yes, I'm sure." And after a few seconds, she sighed. "Never mind, I'll be there in a few minutes." She hung up. "I have to hurry over to the laundry, your father can't find anything." She looked torn.

Debra got up. "It's okay, Mom, I have to get to school anyway. We'll talk tonight." She gathered her books and started out.

"Debra?"

"Yes, Mom?"

"What I was saying earlier, when you asked how I felt when I met your father, dizzy and all that . . . is that how you feel about Steve?"

With her back to her mother, Debra spoke softly. "No."

Sharon paced the corridor behind the *Video High* studio. Every few seconds, she checked her watch. Where *were* those damned skin-heads? She had everything planned, down to the minute. She'd even managed to empty the backstage area so she could keep them hidden until it was time for them to go on.

Normally, all the guests would be back here now. But she'd convinced Steve, Debra, and David Philby to remain in the studio, and wait there while Kris conducted her short interview with Howard. Kris and Howard were already in place on the set. Jeff was showing Dr. Parsons, the board of education panelist, around the studio. Any minute now, Tyler would show up. He'd be doing the introductions and handling the audience questions. She was waiting for the last minute to give him the names of the two additional panelists.

She slipped her hand into her jeans pocket to make sure the note was still there, with the names of the Pro-White Union members who would be on the show. Denny Banks and Kurt Rhodes. Tyler was going to drop his teeth when he saw those names.

She didn't want to think about that, any more than she wanted to think about Jeff Russell's response when he saw the skinheads on the stage. Jeff would be furious. But when he realized how good the show would be, he'd forgive her, just as he'd done before when she went over his head. The ends justified the means, she reminded herself.

The door leading from the studio opened and Tyler came in. "All set?" he asked.

"Almost," she replied. "Um, there's a

change you need to make in the introductions. I've got some more names here." She reached into her pocket.

"I'm not doing the intros today," Tyler told her. "Zack's taking my place."

Her eyes widened. "Why?"

Tyler shrugged. "I don't know. He asked me if he could do it this afternoon. He didn't tell me why, but he sounded urgent. Maybe his father's going to be watching, or something like that, and he wants to be seen."

Sharon's stomach started churning. *She* knew why Zack wanted to be on stage, and in control of the microphone. So he could make sure his racist buddies got lots of support. Those Pro-White guys, they were probably all over the audience, and Zack would make sure they all had a chance to air their views.

She glanced down the hall at the other door, one that led into another corridor. She'd told Denny and Kurt to come in that way, so no one, especially Jeff, would see them pass through the studio.

Then she realized Tyler was gazing at her oddly. "Are you okay? You seem awfully jumpy."

"I'm fine," she said quickly. "Why don't you go out into the studio and get a good seat?"

"All right," he said, but he didn't move fast

enough. The door behind him opened and the skinheads came in.

"We're here," Denny announced unnecessarily.

Tyler stared at them. "You're here for what?"

"We're gonna be TV stars," Kurt declared.

"I told you to come in the back way!" Sharon exclaimed. "Oh, never mind." She went into action. "I want you to wait in here, until I call you." She directed them down to the little storage room at the end of the hall. She practically shoved them both in there and closed the door.

When she turned and faced Tyler, she could barely meet his eyes. He was looking at her in total, utter disbelief.

"What do you think you're doing?" he asked.

"I'll tell you later," she said in a rush. But he didn't move, and his eyes demanded an explanation.

"Look, it's for the good of the show," Sharon said. "This will make *Video High* history, Tyler. It could be the most important show we ever did! African Americans and racists coming face to face, confronting each other! A real, open, and honest discussion!"

"Or a real disaster," Tyler shot back. "Sharon, I can't believe you did this. You can't make decisions like this on your own!"

"I *had* to," Sharon replied stubbornly. "I

know it's right, even if no one else could see that. Tyler, *please* don't let Jeff know they're here." She hurried to the studio door and peered out the window. "Where's Zack? I need to make sure he knows what to say."

Tyler was shaking his head wearily. "Sharon, you have to listen to me."

"There isn't time," she said, but he went on anyway.

"I admire your passion and your commitment, and I know you think you're doing the right thing. But you haven't thought this through, you haven't looked at the possibilities of what this could lead to. This could get you into some real trouble!"

Sharon could feel beads of perspiration forming on her forehead. "I'm willing to take that risk," she said.

His voice rose. "Did you ever consider the fact that this could get all of us into a lot of trouble?"

"What do you mean by that?" she asked. But before he could reply, Zack walked into the area. Tyler caught the swinging door, and held it. Then he looked back at Sharon. "Be careful, Sharon," he said. There was more than a hint of sadness in his voice. "I think this time you've really gone too far." And then he walked out.

Silently, Sharon reached into her pocket and pulled out the slip of paper.

Zack took it from her. "These are the additional panelists?"

"Yes," Sharon said. Zack started back into the studio. "Wait," Sharon called. "Zack, I know why you're doing this."

Zack turned. "Do you?" he asked. "I don't."

He really didn't know why he was standing here, on the stage, in front of the podium, waiting for Jeff to give the cue. Until that day, he'd planned to hide in the back row during the *Video High* taping. Or not come to the taping at all. After all, that was the coward's way out, and he was a coward. That's what his father said.

But some crazy urge had led him to ask Tyler for this job. For some reason, he needed to be here, to be in the middle of it all. Maybe he wanted to be in the middle so he could see both sides, and figure out where he belonged.

His eyes scanned the room. The studio was full. In the front row, Frank and another skinhead were sitting, and they were grinning at him. He pretended not to see them.

The lights over the audience dimmed, and the stage lights came on. The camera lit up. "Action!" Jeff called.

"Good afternoon," Zack said, "and welcome to another edition of *Video High*. We think we have a very interesting show for you today. First off, Kris Hogan will be interviewing Greenwood student body president Howard Weller, who was recently awarded the honor of being selected as *Metro Magazine*'s Outstanding Senior. Kris?''

He waited for the camera to shift away from him, and then he stepped aside. Kris began by extolling Howard's virtues, and then settled into asking him about his accomplishments.

Zack only half-listened. He was studying Kris as she spoke. He'd expected her to drool and fawn all over Howard, and she did, a little. Grudgingly, he had to admit Howard was handling it pretty well, answering the questions simply and directly. If Kris's gushing embarrassed him, it didn't show.

And she looked so pretty, she could get away with anything. Zack felt an ache in his heart as he watched Kris gazing up at Howard, her head tilted pertly to one side, her smile radiant. She used to smile at *him* like that. If it hadn't been for his father, she'd still be smiling like that at him. She was the first girl he'd ever really cared about. And she'd liked him, too, he knew that. She'd be his girlfriend today, if his father hadn't put a stop to it.

He wished he could shut out a small voice inside of him that was saying, "no, it wasn't your father's fault. It was your fault. Because you're a coward.''

The sound of applause broke into his reverie. The interview was over. Jeff yelled "Cut!'' Sharon hurried onto the stage, dragging more chairs with her.

Audience members were standing and stretching, and there was a low rumble of conversation while the stage was arranged for the next segment. "Stevenson," someone hissed. Zack turned and faced Frank.

"Keep that microphone close," the skinhead said. "I got plenty to say." His beady eyes glinted dangerously.

Zack forced himself to make a slight, non-committal shrug. Then he stepped back up onto the stage and behind the podium. He watched as Sharon brought the woman from the board of education onto the stage. She was followed by Debra and Steve and David Philby. There were still two chairs to be filled. Zack glanced at Jeff Russell. He was talking to the cameraman, and hadn't noticed the vacant chairs.

Sharon had disappeared backstage. When she returned, it was with Kurt and Denny. The audience hadn't settled down yet, but a murmur went up from the ones who were watching.

Zack's eyes surveyed the people already seated on the stage. The board of education lady was staring at the skinheads in consternation. Howard and David had their heads bent together, and both shot worried looks at the two new panelists. Steve had edged his chair closer to Debra, and they both looked alarmed, too.

Kurt and Denny were oblivious to this. They

were sprawled in their chairs, looking very pleased with themselves.

Sharon had taken her seat, and she was twisting her hands together. The lights over the audience went down, and finally, Jeff turned around.

Even in the dim light, Zack could read the advisor's face. First, there was shock. That turned to anger. And then the anger dissolved into a grim expression of resignation.

"Action," he barked.

Zack read from Tyler's notes. "All across the country, there have been increasing outbreaks of interracial conflict among adolescents. Today, Sharon Delaney will lead a discussion of race relations in our high schools. Our panelists are student body president Howard Weller, Dr. Danielle Parsons of the Board of Education, David Philby, president of the African American Students League, Steve Nowicki, and Debra Lewis . . ." That was where Tyler's notes ended. Zack filled in the rest. ". . . and two members of the Pro-White Students League, Denny Banks and Kurt Rhodes."

Sharon began. "Thank you all for being here. I'd like to begin by asking David Philby if the African American Students League believes that black students experience discrimination in school."

"We don't feel that there is any institutionalized racism here," David said. "But there is definitely a social and cultural segregation which—"

Denny broke in. "You're damn right there is. We can't keep you people out of our schools, but we don't have to hang out with you."

David continued as if Denny hadn't spoken. "Our feeling is that a lack of communication exists between races which causes misunderstandings, and if we could all become closer—"

This time, it was Kurt who interrupted. "How close do you want to get? Like them?" He pointed to Steve and Debra. "That's what it leads to, you know. Mongrelization of the races!"

Dr. Parsons gasped, and Sharon was looking very nervous.

"Please don't interrupt," she said to Kurt and Denny. "You'll have a chance to air your views. Right now, I'd like to ask Dr. Parsons how we can address the misunderstandings David spoke of. Is the Board of Education concerned about the lack of communication that exists between racial groups?"

"Of course we are," Dr. Parsons replied. "In an effort to ensure more positive attitudes, the Board is currently instituting a multicultural curriculum for the elementary schools. We hope this will teach children about the need to be aware of other people and understand their needs."

"We already understand your needs," Kurt declared. "You want to take over!"

"Yeah," Denny said. "Maybe you can put that kind of multicultural garbage over on grammar school kids, but you can't fool us with that crap."

Dr. Parsons stiffened, and Howard Weller spoke up. "I think we'd all prefer that you don't use obscenities."

"Please don't use obscenities," Denny mimicked in a high-pitched voice. "Where'd *you* learn that fancy language, boy?"

"He must have heard it somewhere," Kurt said. "They can teach monkeys to talk now, you know."

Zack glanced at the audience. They were hushed, and he could feel the tension. He looked at Sharon. He could see that she was struggling to maintain her composure.

"Howard, as a student leader, did you feel that your race presented any obstacles to your success?"

Howard didn't even get a chance to open his mouth. "Are you kidding?" Denny yelled. "Why do you think he *won* that award? Because he's black!"

"Outstanding senior," Kurt snorted. "What a joke."

Sharon's voice was shrill. "Please, let our other panelists speak!"

Someone from the audience rose. "Hey, Weller, are you just going to sit there and listen to those racist pigs?"

Howard spoke evenly. "I don't want to dignify their remarks with a response."

"Maybe he can't come up with one," Kurt declared. "Why don't you go back to Africa where you belong?"

A murmur went through the audience. Dr. Parsons stood up and spoke to Sharon. "I'm sorry, young lady, but I cannot remain here and expose myself to this kind of talk. Excuse me." She walked off the stage.

The murmur in the audience grew louder. Now it was more like a rumble. Sharon looked as if she was close to tears. Zack actually found himself feeling sorry for her. He remembered the microphone he was holding, and spoke into it. "Let's get some comments from the audience."

He spotted some hands flying up, and started in the direction of one. But he didn't get far. Frank jumped up and pulled the microphone toward himself. "Tell us about the Pro-White Union, Denny."

"The Pro-White Union was formed to support white people and promote white pride and keep the races separated," Denny said. "We're sick of being stepped on by inferior people."

"White people unite!" Kurt yelled out.

Now, the audience really came alive. Loud boos could be heard from every section.

Denny's face turned red. "What's the matter with you people? You want to see white girls going out with big black animals?" He jerked his thumb toward Steve and Debra. "You think white guys ought to hang out with black sluts like her?"

Steve jumped up. "Don't you dare talk like that!"

Denny leaped to his feet. "I can say anything I want, man!"

Zack couldn't be sure who struck first. But suddenly, Steve and Denny were rolling around on the floor. Kurt jumped in, too. Debra screamed. Howard and David rushed over and tried to wrench the boys apart. Jeff ran up onto the stage.

Sharon was frozen in her seat. But there was chaos in the audience. Practically all of them were on their feet, trying to see what was going on. A couple of guys ran up to the stage and joined in the fray. Some people were yelling, encouraging the fight, while others were trying to get out of the studio. Zack stood there, unsure of what to do. Dimly, he was aware of the camera panning the scene.

A skinny black kid, who couldn't have been more than a freshman, brushed by Zack, trying to get out. He had the misfortune of colliding with Frank.

Aghast, Zack saw Frank whirl around and knock the kid down. As the boy fell backward, Frank appeared ready to jump on him. Flinging the microphone away, Zack moved between them and pushed Frank back.

"What the hell do you think you're doing?" Frank screamed. He shoved Zack aside. The kid on the floor pulled off his cracked glasses and started to stagger up. Frank lunged at him. Once again, Zack stepped between them, and this time, his fist flew into Frank's face.

There was no mistaking the rage in Frank's expression. Zack braced himself for a punch. But some teacher had appeared behind Frank, and grabbed his arms before Frank could retaliate.

At the same time, Zack was aware of someone gripping his own arms. Half turning his head, he recognized one of the athletic coaches. And along with other fighting students, he was pushed toward the door.

"You're in serious trouble, fellow," the coach snarled in his ear.

"I know, I know," Zack muttered. But strangely enough, he didn't care. The memory of his fist making contact with a skinhead's jaw had him feeling better than he'd felt in ages.

Eleven

Sharon drove her car into the Greenwood parking lot Friday morning and for once, she had no difficulty finding a parking space. There was an obvious reason for that. She was thirty minutes early.

She turned off the engine, but she didn't get out of the car right away. On the one hand, she was anxious to know what was going on, how the school administration had responded to yesterday's *Video High* disaster. On the other hand, she dreaded facing her friends. If she could still call them her friends after what had happened.

Vivid pictures filled her mind. Dr. Parsons walking off the stage. Figures rolling around on the floor. Students being hauled out by teachers. She could still hear Jeff yelling, trying to be heard over the audience, announcing that this week's episode of *Video High* was canceled. She could see Debra's frightened face, Steve's rage, Jeff's grim anger. And Tyler's expression of horrified disapproval.

He hadn't called her last night at his usual

time. She'd sat there by the phone, watching it, checking every now and then to make sure it worked. She'd considered calling him, but she was afraid he'd hang up on her. When he hadn't called by eleven o'clock, she knew he was even angrier than she'd thought. What made the realization worse was knowing he had every right to be.

Her parents had called her out of the room, with the announcement that Greenwood High was featured on the evening news. She'd joined them in the living room, where she was forced to relive the awful experience.

"A violent confrontation ensued during the taping of *Video High* this afternoon," the reporter intoned.

She wanted to look away but the images held her like a magnet. The *Video High* cameraman had caught the whole ugly mess. There was the scene on the stage, with Steve and Denny slugging it out. Then the camera moved to the audience, and she saw something she'd missed that afternoon.

One of those creepy skinheads was about to leap onto some small black kid. Another white guy blocked him, and punched the skinhead before he could make his move. For a second, the white guy's head turned toward the camera, and Sharon was startled to see that it was Zack.

"Sharon, how awful that must have been for you," her mother had said.

Her father was sympathetic, too. "Those bums ruined your show."

Sharon hadn't said much in response. She didn't want her parents to know that the whole catastrophe had been her fault.

But she couldn't hide that fact from her *Video High* colleagues. By now, they would all know that she'd invited the skinheads to be on the show. And she had to face the consequences of her actions.

She got out of the car and went into the school building. There were only a couple of early birds in the entrance area, and she spotted Debra right away. She hurried over to her, and the words tumbled out of her mouth.

"Deb, I'm so sorry about yesterday. I had no idea it would turn out like that. Can you forgive me?"

Thank goodness, Debra wasn't the kind of person who held a grudge. At least, she didn't seem terribly angry. If anything, her reaction was vague.

"Of course," she murmured. Sharon wasn't even sure her words had registered.

"You're not angry?" she asked.

Finally, Debra's eyes seemed to focus. "No," she said, a little sadly. "I'm not angry. I know you didn't want that to happen." She paused, and then added, "I'm not sure how Steve feels about it though."

Sharon winced. "Was he hurt in the fight?"

"No, not really. A couple of bruises. But he

was ordered to appear in Mr. Quimby's office this morning, along with all the other guys who were fighting." She glanced toward the corridor which led to the administration offices. "He's there now."

Sharon groaned. She knew what a summons to Quimby's office meant. Detention, suspension . . . he'd even been known to expel a student for certain major infractions.

"Here he comes now," Debra said.

Sharon turned. Watching Steve approach, she examined his expression. He didn't look terribly distraught.

"What happened?" Debra asked anxiously.

"One week's suspension," Steve replied. He almost sounded cheerful about it.

Debra certainly wasn't. "Steve, that will go on your permanent record! It could hurt your chances for college!"

"I know," Steve said. "But it was worth it." He drew himself up proudly. "I was standing up for something I believe in. You and me."

Sharon had never heard anything so romantic in her life. Steve was willing to sacrifice his future for love!

But Debra didn't seem enthralled by the gesture. If anything, she looked even sadder. "What are you going to do now?"

"Go home," Steve said. "Call my parents at work and break it to them. Look, could you pick up my homework assignments for me? I don't want to get too far behind."

Debra nodded. "I'll come by after school."

Sharon watched him walk out of the building. "At least he doesn't hate me."

"No," Debra said. "You gave him an excuse to do something noble."

"But doesn't that make you feel good?" Sharon asked hopefully. She wanted to believe that *something* positive had come out of this.

Debra didn't respond. She had that dazed expression on her face again. And now Sharon was distracted. Tyler was coming into the building.

She tried to smile as he approached them, but his expression discouraged her. Before she could apologize, he spoke.

"I just saw Jeff Russell in the parking lot. Quimby called him last night and told him he wouldn't be the *Video High* advisor anymore. Quimby said he was holding Jeff personally responsible for what happened on yesterday's show."

Sharon felt like she'd been kicked in the stomach. She couldn't speak.

His announcement brought Debra out of her fog. "But that's not fair! It wasn't his fault."

Tyler's eyes remained on Sharon. "No, it wasn't."

Sharon was drowning in waves of shame. "I didn't mean for this to happen," she said brokenly. She knew she was crying, because Tyler's face became blurry. "You can say it," she whispered.

"Say what?" he asked.

" 'I told you so.' "

His voice was gentle. "I don't need to, do I?"

"Isn't there anything we can do to help Jeff?" Debra asked.

Tyler had no answer, and Sharon didn't need one. Her own conscience provided the response. She turned away from her friends and headed toward the administration offices.

In the assistant principal's office, she asked to see Mr. Quimby.

"He's with someone right now," the secretary told her. "Have a seat." She rolled her eyes. "Or maybe I should say, 'take a number.' "

Sharon saw what she meant. There were two other people in the office—Kurt and Denny. They both glared at her. She found a seat as far from them as possible.

She wondered if this could be the hardest thing she'd ever done in her life. She'd never been in trouble at school before. She could probably avoid it now, too, by keeping her mouth shut. But she couldn't do that. She'd never be able to face Tyler, Jeff, Debra, any of them. Or herself.

She just hoped she wouldn't have to wait too long. The more time she had to think about what she was going to do, the harder it would be.

The door to Quimby's office opened, and Zack came out. He looked a little pale, but composed.

He looked at Sharon, but she couldn't read any accusation in his expression. "What happened in there?" she asked him.

"I got a week's suspension for fighting," he told her, but like Steve, he didn't seem particularly upset by that.

"I saw what you did, on the news last night," she said. "I was surprised."

"So was I," he admitted. He started out.

"Zack?"

He turned back. "Yeah?"

"You're not the guy I thought you were."

He smiled slightly. "That's almost exactly what my father said last night." And then he left.

Zack walked out to the parking lot and got into his car. Glancing in the rearview mirror, he realized he was still smiling. Amazing, when he could still recall his father's reaction to the evening news on TV the night before. And he could anticipate another burst of fury when the senator learned about his suspension.

But he knew he could handle it today, just like he'd handled it last night, and maybe that's why he was smiling. He'd take his father's verbal abuse, and know that it was coming from his father's disappointment that he,

Zack Stevenson, was not a clone of his father. He could even sympathize with his father's frustration. It used to be a source of frustration for him, too.

It had been a revelation to him last night, when his father had bellowed, "How do you expect to follow in my footsteps when you pull a stupid stunt like that?"

The response came from somewhere deep in Zack's heart. "I don't expect to follow in your footsteps. I'm not like you. I'm somebody else."

To which his father had responded with a sneer, "And just who are you, then?"

And Zack had replied, "I don't know. That's what I have to figure out."

The strangest feeling had come over him at that moment—as if he'd been shackled, handcuffed, and now . . . well, he couldn't say the handcuffs had completely disappeared. But they were definitely looser.

No, he didn't yet know who he was. But as he drove out of the parking lot, he had a feeling he was on his way to finding out.

"Mr. Quimby will see you now," the secretary announced.

Sharon went into the inner office. Mr. Quimby was sitting behind his desk, and he looked up irritably. "Yes, what do you want? I'm very busy."

"It's about the *Video High* taping yesterday," Sharon began.

"Were *you* in the fight?"

"No, but—"

"I'm not interested in hearing you defend your violent friends." The assistant principal rose and went to the door.

"But Mr. Quimby—"

He opened the door. "Out!"

"I beg your pardon?" Dr. Moorhead was standing there.

"Dr. Moorhead!" Sharon was relieved. "Please, listen to me. I was on *Video High* yesterday, and—"

"And she's trying to get her friends off the hook," Mr. Quimby finished.

"That's not true!" Sharon exclaimed.

Dr. Moorhead spoke kindly. "Dear, Mr. Quimby's very busy today dealing with the students who were fighting. If you weren't among the students involved in the fighting—"

"But I was!" Sharon interrupted. "I mean, I wasn't actually throwing punches. But I'm the one responsible for the whole thing! Mr. Russell didn't want those skinheads on the show. No one did. I went over his head and invited them myself."

Dr. Moorhead came in and closed the door behind her. "All right, Sharon. Let's hear your story."

The principal's face had become stern, and

Mr. Quimby was glowering. But somehow, Sharon managed to pour out the whole story.

"So you see," she finished, "it was all my fault."

Dr. Moorhead was silent for a moment, and then she nodded. "I agree. I don't believe you can be held completely responsible for the actual violence. It was the individual student's decision to use physical force. But your actions did instigate the situation. Wouldn't you agree, Mr. Quimby?"

The assistant principal grunted. "Perhaps. But Russell should have had more control over his students."

Dr. Moorhead disagreed. "He can't be expected to know what a student has done behind his back. He can't be held responsible for immature behavior or thoughtless actions when he was unaware of them."

Sharon bowed her head. Hearing herself described this way was humiliating. But she couldn't deny one word of it.

Dr. Moorhead continued. "I appreciate your honesty in coming forward with this information, Sharon. But we still must consider an appropriate penalty for your actions. Do you have any thoughts on this, Mr. Quimby?"

The assistant principal looked like a dog who'd just been offered a particularly delicious bone. He *loved* meting out punishments. He was practically licking his lips.

"Well, let's see. There are specific grounds

for suspension. Fighting, theft, cheating, defamation of school property . . ." He looked hopefully at Dr. Moorhead. "Could we fit her crime into one of those categories?"

Dr. Moorhead looked thoughtful. "I don't know if suspension is appropriate. My philosophy is that the punishment should fit the crime." She looked at Sharon. "It was your decision to change the format of *Video High*. Obviously, the program means a great deal to you and you want to have a lot of input. Therefore, I think you should be deprived of that opportunity for a period of two months."

Mr. Quimby agreed, but with reluctance. Sharon had a feeling he would have preferred to see her hung from the school flag pole.

"What about Mr. Russell?" she asked. "Can he keep his position as advisor now?"

"That's Mr. Quimby's decision," Dr. Moorhead said.

Sharon turned to Quimby. All he said was, "You are dismissed." She left the office, went out into the hall, and leaned against the wall.

Quimby had never liked *Video High*. He didn't like Jeff Russell either. So what she had just done, it might have been for nothing.

No, that wasn't true. She hadn't only come here to save Mr. Russell. Just yesterday at this time, she'd been fantasizing about all the credit she'd get for *Video High*. Now, she was obligated to accept the blame.

They said confession was good for the soul. How did her soul feel now?

It still hurt. But at least she'd taken a step toward healing her conscience.

"Where's Sharon?" Jade asked Debra. They had met at Debra's locker after the last bell.

"She went to look for Jeff Russell. So she could apologize."

"Poor Sharon," Jade sighed. "She meant well."

" 'The road to hell is paved with good intentions,' " Debra quoted.

"Good grief, what's that supposed to mean?" Jade asked.

"It's something my father says," Debra told her. "I think it means that trying to do good just might lead you into the wrong direction."

"That sounds about right for Sharon," Jade commented. "What's all that?" She nodded toward the unusually large stack of books Debra was carrying.

"I got Steve's assignments from his teachers."

Jade shuddered. "It was awful, seeing him in that fight, but it must have given you a thrill. I've never had a guy fight for me before."

"You think he did it for me?" Debra asked thoughtfully.

"Who else?"

" 'The road to hell is paved with good intentions,' " Debra repeated. Jade looked at her in puzzlement, but Debra didn't elaborate. "Here comes Sharon."

She'd never seen her best friend looking so miserable. "Did you find Jeff?" Debra asked.

"No, he wasn't in his office."

"We'll find him," Jade assured her. "Let's go wait in the entrance hall."

But before they could set off, Kris Hogan ran up to them. Unlike the others, she wore a big smile. "Did you guys see the news last night?" she bubbled. "We're famous!"

"Great," Sharon muttered. "Just what I wanted to become famous for. Starting a brawl."

Kris was oblivious to her tone. "And did you see Zack? Some skinhead was trying to slug a kid, and Zack jumped in to protect him!" She sighed. "He was so brave. I never thought he had guts like that! I've been looking for him all day to tell him."

"He's been suspended," Sharon told her.

"Really?" Kris looked thoughtful. "Maybe he needs someone to get his assignments. I'm going to call him." She skipped off.

"Well, you made *her* happy," Jade commented.

Debra clutched Sharon's arm. "There's Jeff Russell."

He was coming up the hall with Tyler. When they saw the girls, they crossed the hall to meet them.

"Did you hear the good news?" Tyler asked.

"I've been reinstated," Jeff told them. He focused on Sharon. "That couldn't have been easy for you, going to see Mr. Quimby. He told me you're off the show for two months."

"Maybe I should resign completely," Sharon offered. "I made a mess of things for all of you." She looked at Jeff anxiously.

"No, we need your passion and commitment, Sharon," Jeff said. "You want to change the world, and that's good. But you have to be careful how you go about doing it. The ends don't always justify the means. The means can lead you to an end you don't want."

"I know that now," Sharon said humbly. "I've learned my lesson. I just wish so many people hadn't been made to suffer for it. I feel like *I* should suffer more. Two months' suspension from *Video High* doesn't seem like enough."

"Don't worry about that," Tyler said cheerfully. "I'll keep you informed about what we're doing, and you'll be so jealous, you'll suffer plenty."

That actually brought a smile to Sharon's lips.

Debra was watching Tyler. He was gazing at Sharon with warmth and affection. And something more, too. Understanding. An appreciation for who she was—not who he wanted her to be.

Sharon was telling Jeff she wanted to write

a note of apology to the others on the panel, and they were all making suggestions about what she could say. Nobody noticed as Debra backed away.

Twelve

It was a short walk to Steve's house. He opened the door, and his face lit up when he saw her. "I'm so glad you're here," he said simply.

He moved as if to kiss her, but she bypassed him. "I brought your assignments," she said, laying them down on a table.

"Thanks," he said, and came toward her again. She shook her head.

"What's wrong?" he asked.

She wasn't sure how to begin, so she avoided his question and asked one of her own. "What did your parents say about your suspension?"

"I haven't told them yet," he admitted. "I decided I'd wait till they get home. But I think they'll understand why I had to slug that guy."

"Why *did* you slug Denny?" Debra asked.

He looked at her in surprise. "The jerk insulted you! You're my girlfriend. I had to defend you."

Debra shook her head. "You weren't defending me, Steve. You were defending an idea."

"What do you mean?"

She tried to organize her thoughts. "You believe that people have the right to love each other, no matter who they are. And that no one has the right to break up a relationship. And if a white boy and a black girl are in love, that's okay."

"What's wrong with that?" Steve asked.

"Nothing, absolutely nothing," she assured him. "But Steve—we're not in love. We never were."

Steve stiffened. "How can you say that?"

She wanted to be kind. "You're in love with the idea of being in love. You liked the idea of the two of us together, fighting the world. Steve, I'm not an idea. We're not a symbol. We're two people who like each other a lot. But we let everyone else, our friends and our enemies, force us into being a couple."

Steve sank down into a chair. He rubbed his forehead. "But you—you went along with it, too."

"I know," she said sadly. "I guess I was in love with an idea, too. The idea of having a boyfriend. And you're such a nice guy, it wasn't all that hard to pretend I was in love with you. We were both pretending, Steve. Playing Romeo and Juliet."

Steve rose and paced the floor. "Are you saying I got suspended for nothing?"

"No! It wasn't for nothing, Steve. That creep was saying vile, racist things, and you reacted the way you did because you hate racism. Look, I know physical force isn't the way to solve anything. But it was a natural response. You were standing up for what you believe in!"

Steve gave her an abashed look. "Actually," he said, "Denny hit first." He sat back down on the sofa.

Debra sat down next to him. "Even better!" she declared. "It was self-defense! Let's get hold of the videotape, and show Mr. Quimby. I'll bet we can get your suspension called off."

Steve actually smiled. "I sort of like the idea of everyone thinking it was a romantic gesture. That I slugged him because he called you a slut."

"It *was* a romantic gesture," Debra insisted. "It was beautiful. You were defending love!"

"But not *our* love," he said quietly.

She moved closer to him, and laid a hand on his arm. "No. Not our love. And you know that as well as I do."

They sat there in silence for a moment. "Are you happy right now?" he asked suddenly.

"Not particularly," she said. "I feel . . . sort of sad."

"So do I," he said. "I don't understand how this happened. I wanted us to be this wonderful happy couple, because . . ."

"Because everyone else thought we were," Debra finished. "And we had to live up to their expectations. To show them we could make it, despite all the obstacles."

"And look where we are now," Steve said. "Miserable."

And for the third time that day, Debra thought about good intentions.

"I still care about you," Debra said.

"We're still friends?" Steve asked.

"Absolutely," she said. "And I'd rather have a real friendship than a fake romance."

"It's not exactly *Romeo and Juliet,*" he sighed.

"No, but remember how they ended up," she reminded him.

He looked at her blankly. "Huh?"

"They killed themselves, Steve!"

"Oh, yeah. I forgot about that."

She laughed. Then, impulsively, she leaned over and kissed him on the cheek. He responded with a hug.

Once again, it felt cozy and comfortable. But this time, she had no sense of confusion. This was just the way a hug from a good, dear friend should feel.

About the Author

Marilyn Kaye is an associate professor in the Division of Library and Information Science, St. John's University, and the author of over fifty books for young people.

CAN YOU SOLVE IT?

Use the clues on the cover to solve the mystery . . .
Then, break the seal on the final chapter to reveal the truth!

WHEN YOU HAVE GIRL FRIENDS —
YOU HAVE IT ALL!

Follow the trials, triumph, and awesome adventures of fiv
special girls that have become fast friends in spite of — or be
cause of their differences!

Janis Sandifer-Wayne,	a peace-loving, vegetarian vetera of protests and causes.
Stephanie Ling,	the hard-working oldest daughte of a single parent.
Natalie Bell,	Los Angeles refugee and street smart child of an inter-racial mar riage.
Cassandra Taylor,	Natalie's cousin and the sophisti cated daughter of an upper-middl class African-American family.
Maria Torres,	a beautiful cheerleader who's th apple of her conservative parent' eye.

They're all juniors at Seven Pines High. And they're doing
things their own way — together!

GIRLFRIENDS #1: DRAW THE LINE   (4350, $3.50)
by Nicole Grey

GIRLFRIENDS #2: DO THE RIGHT THING   (4351, $3.50)
by Nicole Grey

GIRLFRIENDS #3: DEAL ME OUT   (4352, $3.50)
by Nicole Grey